Coaching Christine

by
Alex Morgan

© 2006 Alex Morgan
First Edition
10 9 8 7 6 5 4 3 2 1

All rights reserved. No part of this book may be reproduced, stored in a retrieval system, or transmitted, in any form or by any means, electronic, mechanical, photocopying, recording, or otherwise, without the prior written permission of the publishers or author.

The publishers have made every effort to trace the copyright holders but if they have inadvertently overlooked any, they will be pleased to make the necessary arrangements at the first opportunity.

If you have bought this book without a cover you should be aware that it is "stolen" property. The publishers and author have not received any payment for the "stripped" book, if it is printed without their authorization.

All LMH titles, imprints and distributed lines are available at special quantity discounts for bulk purchases for sales promotion, premiums, fundraising, educational or institutional use.

Cover Design by: Leequee Design
Edited by: Charles-Anthony Moore/K. Sean Harris
Book Design, Layout & Typesetting by: Sanya Dockery

Published by:
LMH Publishing Limited
7 Norman Road,
LOJ Industrial Complex
Building 10
Kingston C.S.O., Jamaica
Tel: 876-938-0005; 938-0712 Fax: 876-759-8752
Email: lmhbookpublishing@cwjamaica.com
Website: www.lmhpublishingjamaica.com

Printed in the U.S.A.   ISBN 976-8184-98-1

For Daddy

Survival is the name of the game.

In me you see a man alone,
Drinking up Sundays,
And spending them alone.
A man who knows love,
Is seldom what it seems.
Just other peoples' dreams.

Frank Sinatra
(A Man Alone)
© Warner Bros

And as I rode your winding island roads,
From hilltop to the sea,
I saw that you were scarred–
But still, so beautiful to me.

Garfield Nathaniel
(The Island Beauty)

One

Albert adjusted the rear view mirror so he could keep an eye on the couple in the back. He hoped to God that they wouldn't start having sex in his car. If that happened, he'd probably just throw up. Just married or not, this was a taxi — not a hotel room. They waited this long to be together (five months he was told, as if he cared), they should be able to wait another hour or so. That wasn't asking too much, was it? He didn't think it was. But there they were in the back, kissing and groping each other so enthusiastically that Albert couldn't help but wonder if they would make it to Ocho Rios with their clothes on.

Dem betta! He thought and turned slowly in and out of a corner. It was raining so he had to be extra careful as he navigated the steep, winding Mount Rosser Road. He never did like this road or most of Jamaica's more rural roads for that matter. They were just too damned narrow and big cargo trucks were always either labouring in front of you, making heavy groans like they were trying to shit steel, or barrelling down with so much aggression that you did well if they didn't run you off the road. He could remember once he was taking a Canadian lady to Dunn's River and when he started on Mount Rosser, she looked at the precipice on the right and on the footpath they were driving and said, "Why don't you just go on the main road? This shortcut looks dangerous and it's not saving us any time anyway. Everybody seems to be using it."

"This is the main road."

"Oh, well, I guess this is a part of the *Jamaican Adventure* then."

Alex Morgan

"It is, believe me it is."

"Hey m'buddy, could ya step on id a liddle? Can't wait to stop travelling for tha day, know whad ah mean? Damn!" That was the man in the back seat. His name was Trevor. He was Jamaican but had imported an American accent from his travels. The funny thing was, while they were at the airport in Kingston waiting on his wife, he sounded just as Jamaican as a dancehall deejay. Only now that he had his white, American wife ('Albert, Sheila, Sheila this is Albert our chauffeur,") beside him, he was sounding more like he was trying out for a speak-like-an-American contest where the grand prize was a fabulous Green Card. Imagine that! Nut'n but ah American wannabe, Albert thought. Nut'n worse than a damn wannabe. Instead of wannabe, why not jus' be yuh'self yuh damn...kunumunu?

"Awright," Albert said. A quick glance in the rear-view showed Trevor's hand rooting away between Sheila's legs like a puppy just discovering how plush the linen basket was. Sheila wore denim shorts and, it seemed, the zipper was down to let Trevor in. Either that or he was just kneading her plush linen from the outside. Sheila was giggling and moaning as she enjoyed what Trevor offered. She sounded like she really needed a cooling down. Albert smiled to himself as he remembered that Trevor had peppered shrimps while waiting at the airport. He couldn't remember Trevor washing his hands so if that zipper was down, the unfortunate lady would need a totally different kind of cooling down.

They sure seemed nice and happy now, Albert thought. But soon enough they'd end up like everybody else. They would slide downhill and, before they knew it, they'd be like a militia, fighting for a land called *Happiness in Marriage*. They'd fight as a unit at first and if that didn't work (and it hardly ever did) they'd fight to conquer that land as individuals. Eventually, they'd realise that the land just didn't exist and they were probably better off by themselves. That was how it was. Only the really lucky ones had it any other way.

Albert didn't think Trevor loved Sheila either. Trevor needed to make himself into a full American citizen and Sheila was his access card. She was at least ten years older than Trevor and not good-looking. Her personality was nice though, and probably the only reason Albert did not think she was down right ugly. She was more like a bombed-out blond than a blond bombshell. But she did have lively eyes and an infectious come-and-get-it smile. Maybe that smile was a tad too infectious, he thought, and that was why she also looked like she probably had a history of over fifty men coming and getting it — including the college football team that she consented to gangbang her in the locker room after training one rainy Friday afternoon. Maybe.

Back at the airport, Trevor had showed him a picture and said, "Ah she wi ah look out fah."

Albert looked at the picture and smiled as though he really cared a donkey's ass about what she looked like. There were two ladies in the picture, standing in front of a little bar with *Sheila's Hole* written on an American flag just above the door. Albert's eyes automatically selected the younger one for she seemed closer to Trevor's age.

"Sweet, don't?" Trevor said above the cry of aircrafts.

"Is what this she have?" Albert asked, "Red-green hair?"

Trevor looked closer and chuckled sympathetically. "No man," he said, "Ah nuh she dat. She ah di nex' one. Di green hair one ah mi stepdaughtah."

"Oh, oh, oh," Albert went, "Weh yuh ah seh?" He then paid some attention to the other woman. "Mature," he said.

Now as he got another glance at her face as Trevor turned on the heat, Albert was thinking he probably undershot the age a bit. Fifteen years older seemed more like it — if she had done a facelift, it was closer to twenty.

She seemed to be a more genuine person than Trevor though and that alone made her better in Albert's eyes. She didn't say much but she didn't really have to as her come-and-get-it smile and those blue eyes also said that if you were good to her she'd be good to you. Sheila never griped when the car ran into an unavoidable mottle of potholes and just chuckled when some other drivers appeared to want to run them off the road just to get in front. Quite likely, she had been here before and knew very well that this was how some people drove in Jamaica. But Trevor lived most of his life here, Albert figured, yet every time there was a bad overtake he would say, "Oh my God!" in his wannabe American accent.

"Hey m'buddy pud a move on it, uh!" Trevor went in between the kisses, "You're drivin' like you get paid by the hour or somethin'..."

"Me is not yuh buddy," Albert told him. "Buddy mean penis out yah an' me is not yuh penis so don't call me dat."

Silence.

"No shit!' Trevor said and Sheila giggled.

"What's he sayin'?" Sheila asked.

"Buddy means penis out here. Penis! Not cock or dick, but penis. My, my, ain't we brought up proper."

"Yes we is," Albert said, mocking Trevor's tone. He spoke naturally now, "Call mi Albert, ah dat mi name."

"Okay then...Albert could you speed id up a liddle?" Trevor said from behind a snicker.

"Ah will try my best but remember di road wet so ah have to take extra care."

"I understand bud – I mean, Albert. Do what ya must." Trevor snickered again. His voice then fell to a pitch he thought Albert wouldn't hear. "Dickhead," he said, "maybe that's whad I should be callin' him, eh baby? Or cocksucker!"

"Oh, Trev," Sheila said, "don't be like that."

"Don't be like what? The man's a fuckin' freak! Everything ticks him off."

Freak! Yuh waan si freak? He then ground his teeth and sank the gas pedal so fast and hard that it made a popping sound. The car kicked off like a turbo engine was engaged. The raindrops splattered as they hit the windscreen. The snaking road now uncoiled before their eyes as if they were watching a fast-forwarded videotape. Corners seemed nonexistent as the car ploughed through the afternoon rain. Trevor sat bolt upright.

"Hey, take id easy. When I said step on it I didn't mean this fast! Whad are you tryna do, ged us killed or something?"

"Or something," Albert said, unflinching. "Welcome to Jamaica, mon," he added with a sarcastic grin.

The ride continued like this till they were in Ocho Rios. By this, the rain had stopped and the sun was out so bright you wondered if it was some prankster with a whole lot of water that caused the roads and trees to be wet. They actually got there twenty minutes ahead of schedule. Albert was only too happy to get their things from the trunk and land them at the entrance of Eagle Cottages, a mid-priced resort. Albert assumed Sheila would be footing the bill.

Trevor slapped the payment in Albert's hand. Sheila was standing at a desk in the lobby, filling in forms and collecting keys. A wide, straw-coloured hat and a pair of designer sunglasses now protected her from the bright, Jamaican sunshine.

"Ah wha' yuh did ah try do taxi bwoy, flop mi show?" Trevor asked. Sheila was way out of earshot so he could use the patois to sound tough. "Yuh nuh know seh yuh wi dead?"

Albert smiled. "Mi done dead a'ready," he said.

Trevor looked at him for a while without speaking.

"Trev," Sheila called. "Could you give me a minute? I want you to help me decide on something."

He called back at her in a quick change of accent, "Sure, baby." He walked off without looking back at Albert. "Damn freak," he said.

As he got into the car, Albert was hoping he never had to deal with those two again. Well, not Sheila. She was okay, but he suspected wherever she was the damn wannabe would be also. It was such a pity nice people had to come across trash like Trevor.

He was about to start the engine when he looked up and saw her. "Jesus mi God!" He said and swallowed hard.

Two

Jamaican women generally have what could only be described as amazing powers over men. Depending on the woman and her intentions, a man could find himself laughing or sobbing, or coming or going before he realises he isn't even making a conscious effort to do anything. Depending on the woman, a man might also be made to live again! Sometimes, she does it intentionally but there are other times when it just happens, like some meals turn out great while others don't and you really can't explain it for you did the same thing each time. Some people call it chemistry, some allure and others *pum-pum* power. But however it happens or whatever you call it, the man who benefits is usually eternally thankful.

Today, Albert was feeling like such a man.

She was cleaning a room on the first floor. The swimming pool was just below that section of the building and the giant scales of sunlight on the water made it glitter and reflect on the walls like a disco ball. Albert could hear the sea but could not see it, as it was more to the back of the premises. The pleated candy-striped skirt the woman wore danced about her like a hula-hoop as she pushed and turned the mop on the tiles. The air was quite cool but she was sweating twice as much as she should have been. Albert saw her use the back of her hand to wipe her forehead. She momentarily baptized the mop in a yellow bucket close by, and then squeezed out the excess water with a lever contraption fixed to one side of the bucket. As she did this, she had to bend forward a little and his eyes caught some more of her thighs. His forehead started sweating too and he hooked a handkerchief from his pocket and patted it away like a nervous insurance salesman.

Unusually, he was hoping the skirt was a little shorter so he could see some more.

Unusually, because for the past year or so, his sexual senses had been nonexistent — but he was now, not just having an interest but also getting...a rise!

Hallelu-hallelu-hallelu-halleujah! Praise Ye the Lord!

"Jesus mi God!" Albert wiped his lips with the kerchief. He suddenly felt weak, dazed. Could this be true? It is, he thought, it's alive! There was life after that Princess bitch after all.

The pain was still there though. And it was wrenching at his chest even now as he thought of Princess Williams — her sparkling eyes, her intriguing smile, her warmth. The images were all coming back now like they did many nights in his dreams. Those dreams from which he would emerge with a jolt, sweating and shaking violently. Those dreams in which the beautiful woman who smiled at him at the start, turned into a giant pussy toward the end. The pussy had big teeth that were shaped like stalactites in caves. They would gnash at him and the pussy would snarl like a vicious beast. It would come at him, jumping like a woman in a potato sack race, menacing and dripping all over. But though it would come at him and he would be frightened, Albert wouldn't run. He would somehow feel that it would not hurt him. But it would. It always did. In each dream, it bit his cock off at the root and he would wake up convulsive, grabbing his crotch like a blind man feeling around for spilt coins. The pain was still there.

And it was because of this persistent pain why Albert was thinking he probably shouldn't even go on over to the woman and introduce himself. He didn't want to get into that sort of thing again. Not now. Not until he was sure he was ready. A hard penis — ("Not cock or dick, but penis. My, my, my ain't we brought up proper.") — didn't always mean you were ready. Sometimes it meant that you had to be very careful. So he thought about just getting in the car and driving away from here. Drive away and go look for his mother like he planned to do. The sooner he got there, the more time he'd be able to spend with her.

But he couldn't. This woman had done something to him that had not happened in a while and he was forced to respect that. So much so that Albert was feeling very grateful indeed. He couldn't leave like this. The chemistry, allure or pum-pum power was just too strong.

He started for the stairs to where she was. He knew it wasn't love for he couldn't feel that anymore. Princess made sure of that. It was just that the woman seemed so arousing from where he was standing that he felt compelled to get closer. Maybe after getting there, he would realise she wasn't as flaming as she appeared from afar.

"Christine!" A male voice called from somewhere on the ground floor. Albert was now mid-way up the stairs. The woman stopped what she was doing and leaned over the rail of the balcony. "Yes, Missa Shoat?" She said, just loud enough for the person to hear her. Albert heard her too.

"Christine," Albert said to himself. It was by no means an exotic name. He had two cousins with that name and he heard it on the street too often to remember. But now as he said it, the name was like cotton candy on his tongue, soft and sweet. Christine.

"Come yah," Mr. Shoat said.

"Cho, fuck!" Christine said and pushed the wet-mop and bucket into the first empty room. She pulled the door shut behind her. She then locked it and dropped the keys in the apron pockets of her skirt and started toward Albert.

"Hi, Christine," Albert said just as she stepped past him, His expression was a blank stare — perfect for a game of poker. But this wasn't poker...at least not yet.

She looked him over for recognition. None. She didn't know this man and her demeanour reflected this. It said she didn't know him, but she knew his type: weirdo fucks who watched you for days or months without ever saying anything to you. Then one day, after conjuring up all sorts of blissful moments with you in their minds — maybe even jacking off a time or two — they present themselves along the staircase and say corny things like *Hi, Christine.* She knew their type, all right. If you worked at a hotel on the North Coast, they started thinking you were exceedingly liberal and into one-night stands and orgies with every oddball that came by. They assumed you were easy because in their fantasies you were.

"Hi," she managed and stepped away quickly.

Shoat came to meet her at the foot of the stairs. He was short, shirtless and gorilla-hairy. He carried a big gut that made him walk laid back, like a pregnant woman. He glanced up quickly and saw Albert. Apparently, Shoat deduced he was Jamaican — a local — and so was not deserving of a greeting. Albert's keys were in his hand so he probably also figured he was a taxi driver. He was therefore uninhibited as he spoke. "Mi nuh tell yuh seh fi clean numba four so mi can get it fi Missa Goldsrnit'?" Shoat had a high-pitched voice, like a sissy. Albert thought he sounded like a man he knew from somewhere in his childhood only as Den-Den.

"Yes, Missa Shoat," Christine said.

Shoat looked at Albert again and came a little closer to Christine as if to tell her a secret. "Oh! So weh di rass yuh nuh do it? Eeeh, Christine?"

"Because mi si yuh in dere, sar. Mi cyaan clean di room if yuh in it." She spoke in a low pitch, as if embarrassed and didn't want to draw attention to herself.

Shoat licked his lips. He gesticulated as he spoke, his palms up turned like a man begging alms. "But, Christine mi nuh done show yuh a'ready seh if mi inna di room a tek a likkle rest yuh can come in same way cause mi nuh min'? Nuh dat mi tell yuh?"

"Yes sar."

"So why yuh nuh do it den? Yuh fraid? Yuh t'ink mi ah go hold yuh dung in deh?"

Christine didn't answer.

Shoat stepped back like a boxer who got a surprise punch to the face and studied her carefully. "Oh, oh! Soh ah dat yuh t'ink! But what ah raas dis pon mi, eeeh?" He glanced toward the man on the steps. The local. Albert turned his head away and pretended to be admiring the beautiful landscape. Shoat continued, "Is 'bout a million time now mi beg yuh likkle front from yuh come yah an' yuh nuh gi mi none, so wha' mek yuh mus' feel seh mi ah go hold yuh dung an' tek it? Oh, oh! Yuh t'ink me's a rapist? Eeeh?"

"No, Missa Shoat," she managed.

"But is mus' dat yuh tek mi fa to raas! Mek mi tell yuh sop'm, Christine, yuh deh yah fi do di wuk when mi tell yuh fi do it an' how mi tell yuh fi do it. If yuh nuh want it yuh can gwaan back ah Macca Tree. Mi may short but mi nuh short ah pussy to raas." He stepped off, disappearing down a paved footpath that led to the back of the property.

Christine wiped her forehead and turned back for the stairs. As she passed Albert, she grumbled like a wayward child who had just been scolded.

With the bucket and mop in hand, Christine started for the room she was instructed to do pronto. Albert's eyes followed her every step till she got to where she now stood at a white door on the ground floor with a brass '4' on it. He didn't say anything further to her and she did likewise.

Albert got into the car and headed out. He wasn't fully out of Fern Gully when he started feeling stupid and alone.

Three

"An' yuh know Princess was jus' here!" Ester said. She had lost a lot of weight since the mastectomy but if you didn't know her from before, you would have no idea she was battling cancer. You would just think she was rather slim built, for her smile was true and free of the intense pain she felt at times. She coughed frequently but even that wasn't enough to betray the inner peace she seemed to have found. Ester wore a do-rag like a hip-hop fan but it was to conceal the hair loss brought on by chemotherapy. It wasn't for the cool look. The sheet of African print she had for a dress was not a matter of style either. That was to cover some places where the treatment left dark burns.

"Thank God," Albert said. He kissed her on the cheek and sat beside her, throwing one arm over her shoulders and pulled her close to him almost like they were lovers. The TV was on with Jerry Springer introducing yet another domestic brawl. Derrick, his younger brother, was still at work. Ester decided to stay with Derrick as he lived in Stony Hills where it was cooler. Derrick also had a helper. Her name was Rose Fletcher. It was also good that Rose was at the house so Ester would never really be alone when Derrick and his wife were at work. Right now, Rose was in the kitchen preparing dinner. They could sometimes hear her singing a gospel song above the sound of Jerry Springer and his hooligans and the clutter of the utensils she used.

Ester chuckled. "What? Nuh tell mi you two still not talking?"
"Den mama, yuh really expect me fi talk to her afta what she do me?"

COACHING CHRISTINE

"If mi did think like you, you probably wouldn't even born," Ester said.

"How yuh mean?" Albert asked.

"Mi mean dat if me did leave your father an' never talk to him again after him cheat the first two times and me find out, you wouldn't be here today. Now mi nuh sayin' yuh should go back to her but you can at least talk to her. She still come look for me and she an' Derrick talk good-good."

"Well, dat ah you an' Derrick. Me an' her different. She never hurt you nor Derrick like she hurt me."

"People leave people fi other people all the time. Is a part of life till yuh find the one that right for you." She smiled as she reflected. "Even when I started seeing Ralston, I was with somebody else. Ralston jus' come an' thief mi weh from him." Ralston Bench was Albert's father. He died back in '86 in a car accident.

"Ah wha' yuh ah tell mi seh?" Albert went. "But mama yuh did a gwaan bad?"

"An' yuh know di man to yuh nuh," Ester said.

Albert was instantly lit up by all the intrigue. "Me know him? Who dat now?"

"Errol," Ester said and coughed.

"Errol!" Albert pulled away and hung back, reflecting his shock. Errol Gentles was a police officer that used to come by the house many times to look for the family. He always carried little gifts for Albert and Derrick, and had an ongoing domino competition with Ralston, but at no time did Albert get the impression that Errol and his mother were once an item. "Daddy tek yuh way from Errol?"

Ester nodded. "An' yuh see how me an' Errol still talk good? In life, yuh have to be a' adult an' know sen yuh win some an' yuh lose some."

Ester took up the remote and turned off the TV as a fat white woman was holding down a black man to stick her tongue in his mouth and about four men were restraining a raging fat black woman who seemed to want to beat the hell out of both of them.

"So you meet anybody else yet?" Ester asked.

"Mi see a girl today. She look alright..." Albert said.

"That sound good," Ester said and then she started coughing. Rose was quick to hear and came around with a glass of water. Albert took the glass and gave it to Ester who had some. "So when mi goin' to meet her?"

"Soon," he said.

"Ah hope so," she said. "Ah really hope so."

Four

That night Albert had a dream. Dreams were quite usual for him these days. Since the doctor gave him some pills for his depression ("These are to relax you a little. You will sleep well at night. I guarantee it."), he was just having all sorts of really vivid visions. It was like a cinema opened a feature film in his mind every night. They had fabulous three-dimension picture and digital sound. For the most part, they starred Princess who later became that giant pussy which would eat up his manhood. For this reason, when they started — no matter how much they looked like one of those the-world-is-a-wonderful-place scenes from movies like The Sound of Music — he would hold his breath for he was almost certain the terror would come. It was normally a really good horror flick.

But not tonight.

Tonight was different. It wasn't about Princess coming over to hug and kiss him just before her face melted. Christine was featured tonight. She was the leading lady and Albert the leading man. A star.

In this dream, Christine was running away from Den-Den. She was running to Albert's open arms. Den-Den was shouting at her, "Oh! Oh! Yuh ah run from man wid money an' tek up taxi man? Yuh dyam wutless raas, yuh! Yuh t'ink taxi man can gi yuh weh mi can gi yuh?" He dipped into his pocket. Albert could see the impression the arm made under the fabric like an eel was trying to get out. It went all the way to just above the knee and when it came up it held a fist full of US money. One hundred dollar bills, tens, twenties. They resembled Monopoly money but Albert knew they were real. "Mi ha money," Den-Den said. "Mi can buy all ah million zillion taxi. Can all buy yuh to, if mi want, ahoe."

When Christine got to Albert, she collapsed in his arms. This dream was even better than the movies for he could smell the talc she had on, a light musk. Christine buried her face in his chest and cried. "All right," Albert told her, "Come work fi mi now." And he kissed her on the top of her head. Den-Den was still talking but Albert wasn't hearing him anymore. All he heard now was the sound of — (music) — two hearts beating. This was how he woke up. The dream was good and waking up was wonderful. He was now back to the real world where he could attempt to make the dream a reality. If he could just live in the dream forever and ever — then again maybe not, for if the dream went on for longer, Christine might just turn into Princess and crush him again. Maybe she could be a lot worse. The real world could turn out bad or good in just the same way as dreams but at least right now he felt like trying out for some good. God knows he had been in the bad long enough. Quite possibly, it was time for a change.

Christine's face floated in front of him in the dark of the room. It was so clear — like a movie poster with her face in the centre, the rest being a chromatograph of darkness. Albert momentarily wondered if he was still dreaming. He checked the glowing clock on the wall across the room. Its neon green hands were showing a quarter past four. He wondered what Christine was doing now. Was she alone in bed like he was or was she wrapped tightly in the arms of some — "Mi ha' money...Mi can buy all ah million zillion taxi" — man? Was she anything like Princess? Albert could remember back in the eighties at a Labour Party election campaign one of the candidates — it could have been Mike Henry or Edward Seaga or somebody else, he wasn't quite sure now — said, "If a man rob yuh clothes what yuh call him? Ah robbah! An' if him bake bread him is a bakah. So if a man mash up everyt'ing yuh have, him is nutt'n but a damn mashupah! Socialist mash up di country an' dem is a mashupah!" The crowd swelled in jubilation sounding like a stadium full of football fans whose team just scored an all-important goal. Now as Albert thought about Princess, he believed that's really what she was: a mashupah. She mashed a wonderful relationship till it became dirt.

He felt himself getting hard as he remembered Christine bending over to wring the mop, her half dozen or so bangles chattering on her wrist. He saw women every day — some of the most beautiful and attractive women in any man's book. Yet, none was able to affect him like this since Princess left him. It could be that he was just ready to get on with his life. But it could also be that this was the only woman that could get him revved up again. In a way, he felt like Peter must have when Jesus told him to walk on water. Don't look down or have any doubts, man, just keep your eyes on me and you'll be all right. Just walk. Albert wondered if he was now ready to walk again. Would he just sink like a wounded ship or would he stay on top, ride the waves, like those tyre tubes people liked to float on over by Hellshire beach?

Albert thought of trying to reach her by phone but decided not to after picking up the receiver from the night table. She probably didn't even stay at the resort, he thought, and besides, they never met formally. He got her name only because Den-Den shouted it. She quite likely wouldn't remember him either. Not until he reminded her and then she'd remember and hang up, thinking he was some (damn freak) creep who wanted to stalk her. Stalk her like the guy in that Ray Stephens song, *It's Me Again Margaret* (tee, hee, hee. Are you n'kid?). He didn't want to be that guy.

Yuh shoulda talk her up yesterday, man, he thought. *Then yuh woulda get the damn numba. She might all like yuh an' yuh nuh know.*

The thought kept resounding in his mind even as he left for work.

Five

Albert was in Half Way Tree when he finally decided he was going to call the Eagle Cottages. He had saved the number in his cell phone so he took it from its holder on the visor and scrolled through. He found it and dialled but it rang without an answer. He tried again five minutes later. By this, he was going up Hope Road with passengers en route to Papine and Mona. He did this route six days a week provided the Transport Authority people weren't out with their good friends, the cops, taking away cars trying to make a quick dollar in the route taxi business. It was a risky business (if they took the car, it required about twenty grand to get it back) but if he didn't do this, the bills wouldn't get paid. Legal taxi operators were safer from the cops but the licensing fee was greater for those red plates and the tax office wasn't keen on issuing more at this time (The system was currently full. "Try again next year."). Even if you had those red plates – the guys on the stand called them lipstick – and did the route taxi thing up these parts where the bus service was regular, your car could still get towed.

Added to this, route taxiing could potentially pay a lot more than sitting around waiting for some poor soul to holler, "Taxi!" so you could take them down the road for a hundred dollars (or a dollar as the guys called it, reflecting a truer value of its US counterpart). If you were the only one there with the lipstick plates, you would make some good money but when you were there with every man who was made redundant in the country's recent economic collapse – with more every damned day – you could really suffer out there.

So the route taxi business became an option to all — lipstick or no lipstick — at some time or the other. *Damned if you do, damned if you don't,* Albert thought and tried the number again.

"Thank you for calling the Eagle Cottages," a voice said, "Everton Shoat speaking."

Me know seh ah you, Den-Den, Albert thought. The voice could not have missed recognition. It was loud and coarse like an overworked sportscaster's, reporting on a race in which his horse was losing. Though Albert could detect some effort to mask this (just like the customer service manual directed, he supposed) it wasn't working very well. He still sounded like a Den-Den.

"Yes," Albert said, "Good morning, could I speak to Christine?"

Silence.

"She nuh work yah nuh more, yuh nuh," Den-Den said. It seemed he wasn't thinking customer service anymore.

"What? Bu. . .but me see her deh yesterday."

"Mi seh," Den-Den insisted, "Christine nuh work here again. Yestuhdeh is yestuhdeh an tuhdeh is tuhdeh. Two different day. One is yes an' di odda is to."

"Wha' she do, resign?"

"Call it dat," Den-Den said.

"Call it dat?" Albert asked.

"Yeah, call it dat or call it whateva else yuh raas want, but she nuh deh yah!" He was shouting, irritated.

"Is so yuh talk to people? Yuh damn reprobate! What kind ah language dat yuh ah use to me? Yuh mouth want to wash out wid some Jeyes cleaner. Yuh—"

The phone went dead. Albert checked to see if he had lost a signal. Nothing was wrong except the damn jackass of a man had hung up on him. If Ocho Rios wasn't so far, Albert thought, he'd just go up there to let him know how rude he was to even think of doing something like that. He didn't bother to call back now for he knew he probably wouldn't answer. Besides, he had passengers in the car and didn't want them listening in too much on his life. He knew they were listening to him. They always were.

So she wasn't there anymore. What was he going to do now? Just like that, the woman that came into his life like a blessing from God himself was out of it like (people leave people fi other people all the time) — she was never there in the first place. But was she ever? Could he say that of someone he saw once was in his life? If the one meeting was profound enough, he thought he could say that.

If yuh nuh want it, yuh can gwaan back ah Macca Tree.

But of course, Albert thought. Den-Den did indicate Christine was from a place called Macca Tree. He knew of one place called Macca Tree up in St. Catherine near Brown's Hall and Mount Pleasant. He was also aware that there could be a few more places of that name that he didn't know about but he was willing to start with the one he knew and proceed from there. He would go there and ask around. He didn't have her last name and Christine was quite common but so what? There couldn't be that many Christines in Macca Tree anyway. If it had a thousand, he would check them all out until he found the one. It meant that much to him.

That settled it. After dropping off the last person at the University of the West Indies, Albert took the rest of the day off to go find a woman he knew only as Christine.

Six

The first stop Albert made as he entered the rural district of Macca Tree, was a little shop with a sign that said *Ferdie's Sell All* just above its zinc awning. Two old men sat on a bench in the shade of the awning, just looking out at the bright day. Another was seated in the shop, behind the counter. Albert assumed he was Ferdie.

"Sell mi a Pepsi deh, Missa Ferdie," he said as he entered the shop. To his left, about four or five boys in khaki were huddled round a video game of some sort. The game made roaring sounds and it seemed their eyes were stuck to the glowing screen as one of them used his entire body to operate the joystick.

"Bombaaatt!" One of the boys said.

"Hi, hi!" Ferdie called at them. "None of dat inside here. Unnu cyaan behave unnu self, go ah unnu yard." He wore khaki, as well, but his looked as old as he was and had dark stains. *Probably he used to be a farmer. Probably he still was.*

The boys fell silent. Albert could hear air releasing, like one of them was trying hard not to laugh. The silence prevailed though.

It took him a while, but Ferdie eventually got the drink and handed it to Albert. It was like Ferdie could only do things thirty seconds after he decided to. Albert paid him. Ferdie first brought the coins close to his glasses and then he dropped them in what sounded like a huge, empty box beneath the counter.

Albert guzzled some of the drink. He looked across the road just in time to see a man leading a donkey by a rope. The donkey bore hampers that were stuffed with hands of green bananas.

"Mi lookin' fi a girl name, Christine," he said to Ferdie.

"Christine?" Ferdie said after a while.

"Yeah. She 'bout twenty-t'ree or so. Nice looking girl an' she work ah Ochi."

Ferdie thought for a while longer. "Oh yeah man, mi know har. She live roun' deh so. Sweet girl, sweet girl." He pointed to a narrow road leading northwest. It disappeared into what resembled a lane with more trees than houses. A direct contrast to what you'd expect to find in a Kingston lane.

Ferdie slowly came around the counter and followed Albert outside. He never stopped pointing that index finger at the lane. Not once. It was like he forgot he was doing it.

"When yuh go up deh yuh wi' si one house wid a blue awnin' – one ah di tarpaulin one dem."

"Far up?" Albert asked.

"Eh nuh," he said. Albert figured that meant no. "'Bout five minutes walk."

"Thanks," Albert said and got in the car.

As it turned out, the house Ferdie described was no five-minute walk. Well maybe it could be for an athlete with a world record in walking but not for the average man – certainly not for Ferdie. At one point, Albert wondered whether he made a wrong turn somewhere. But then, he remembered he made no turns. He was just driving and looking out for a house with a blue awning. Maybe they took the awning down, he thought. Maybe from ten years ago! Ferdie seemed quite slow and maybe he was still wondering why he wasn't hearing much from Michael Manley these days.

Finally, Albert did see the house with the blue awning but it was the wrong woman. Yes her name was Christine, but she was about twenty-five years older than the Christine he was looking for (compliments of Ferdie's memory jam). The woman wasn't good looking either, Albert thought the house looked a lot better than she did. She wore a wedding band so someone did see something in her at some point (quite likely that's where Ferdie's memory froze). These days she looked like a man with big breasts.

"Sorry," Albert said, "Is somebody else me lookin' for."

"Yuh sure me cyaan help yuh, lover boy?" She asked. She came up to the car and leaned over his door. The tail of her blouse was wet and he could smell detergent on her, like she had been doing laundry.

"Not unless yuh can tell mi if yuh know any other Christine up here," Albert said, ready to speed off if she tried to grab him.

She sighed. "Go back dung di road an' tek di firs' lef. She live at di end ah dah road deh."

"Respect," Albert said.

"Yuh ah run from progress," she told him and went back inside.

Albert turned the car around and drove down the hill as quickly as he could. The first left took him deeper into forestry. There was a single house at the end of the road. It stood there like a mirage. As the car got closer, an old lady emerged from the front door and stood on the veranda. He hoped that was not the other Christine.

Albert parked and got out. "Hello," he said from behind the hibiscus hedges.

"Mornin' missa genkleman," the old lady said. She spoke a little too loud, as though she was in the midst of a buzzing crowd.

"I'm here to see Christine...is she in?"

The lady seemed cautious as she came from the porch and closer to where Albert stood by the hedge. "An' who yuh be, sar?" She was much shorter than Albert and as she spoke she looked up at his face, her eyes squinted as if she were being blinded by the sun's glare.

"My name is Albert Bench. She don't know mi but I'm here to give her a job..."

"Ah si," she said, nodding. She then offered him a hand. "Matilda Victoria Myrie," she said.

"Pleased to meet you, Matilda," Albert said and shook her hand.

"Cho! Call mi Matilda," she said and smiled. Hearing problem confirmed.

Matilda Victoria Myrie went to the small gate and let Albert in. "So is di hotel weh she use' to work sen' yuh?"

This was when he started thinking he was really in the right place. "Not exac'ly," he said, following her lead. "But dem tell mi seh she not working there anymore. I see how she work an' I like what mi see. So seein' that mi have the vacancy, she is the first person that come to mi mind."

"Eh nuh," Matilda said just like Ferdie. "She nuh deh deh nuh more. She seh di man weh own di place did ah put wud to har so she tell him off an' lef."

"Really?" Albert said.

"Christine!" Matilda called as if she didn't hear Albert. "Tan good. Mi have one man yah seh him come fi look fi yuh." Matilda led Albert to the back of the house.

He recognised Christine from behind and instantly felt relieved. She was leaned against the rails of a pigpen, throwing food at the raucous animals. The noise suggested there was a rush on the food, like they were very hungry and she had just started feeding them.

"Christeeeeen!" Matilda hollered. "mi seh mi have a genkleman fi si yuh. Him seh him have wuk fi gi yuh ..." She walked with an evident limp but she didn't seem to need any help getting around. Albert had to make an effort to keep up with her.

Christine looked around. *Finally*, Albert thought. She had a dirty white bucket in her hand. It contained peels of breadfruit, yam and something else Albert thought could very well be clumps of flour. The denim she had on was not filthy but was splashed with juice from the bucket so it looked like the apron of a hard working baker. There was some amount of recognition in her eyes now. She knew she had seen him somewhere before.

"Hi, Christine," Albert said.

"Da's all yuh know fi seh?" Christine asked.

"Smile nuh, pickney! But my God!" Matilda said. "Yuh nuh hear mi seh di genklernan come fi gi yuh wuk?"

Christine forced a smile. It was hardly convincing but it was pretty to look at nonetheless.

"At least yuh remember me," Albert said and chuckled.

"Wha' type a work yuh have?" Christine asked.

Albert fidgeted uncomfortably. "Well yuh know, a little helper t'ing...nut'n much, really. You can stay there durin' di week an' come home on weekend if yuh want. Or yuh can stay there seven days a week. Mi have a spare room not usin' so is no bother really."

"Why me?" She asked.

"Mmm?"

"Why yuh want me?"

"Weeell," Albert said as he thought quickly of what to say. "Me didn't like how Den-Den — mi mean, Missa Shoat — was treatin' yuh an' I just think that if yuh did have a choice yuh coulda leave if yuh want...teach him a lesson."

"Da's right," Matilda said.

Christine put down the bucket and wiped her hand in the denim. "Teach him a less'n?" She said with some amount of contempt. "Ah prison him fi fuckin' go!"

Albert staggered to keep his balance. That one caught him totally off guard. He swallowed hard. "My, my, my. I think we need fi control wi tongue though, Christine. If yuh don't even respect me, have some fi the old lady nuh!"

"Sar, I tell har everyday seh har mout' too dutty an' she fi wash it out wid soap," Matilda said.

Me think so too, Albert thought but said nothing. *Such a foul word comin' from such a sweet looking mout'. Vulgar! Jesus Christ, she sound like the hog dem. Have to bridle her for sure.*

All three of them went back to the house and sat on the veranda's ledge. Matilda brought Albert some lemonade. He found it quite refreshing. Actually, it wasn't lemon or lime that was in it, but a citrus fruit they called *sibble-sweet*. Matilda pointed it out to him on a tree that stood at the centre of a small garden of *Joseph's Coat* to the side of the house. The fruits resembled oranges but the skin was rough and lumpy. They looked nice and ripe hanging there but they were eternally sour and so they were used for nothing more than making the drink.

A girl of no more than ten came from the house and found a seat just behind Christine. She rested her head on Christine's back and plopped a thumb in her little mouth.

"Yuh wake, pumps?" Matilda said and smiled at the little girl.

The child did not reply. Her bright eyes were fixed on the strange man.

"Granny, nuh call har so. Mi tired fi tell yuh. Har name is, Jodi-Ann. If yuh cyaan call har by har name nuh badda call har at all." Christine shuffled and shot out her mouth.

Jus Like di ol' hog dem, Albert thought and smiled.

"Lawks," Matilda said. "Den ah wha' mek yuh so fiery missis?"

Christine said, "But mi tell yuh all di while seh nuh call har so. Call har by har right name, an' yuh still do it!"

"Your likkle girl?" Albert asked after a while. It just came without much thought. He wasn't thinking she had a child (or children! Yikes!), and now that he thought about it, he wondered if he was ready to take some other man's child into his care. He didn't even have a child of his own for Christ's sake.

"Yes," Christine said.

She had a child, so what? Albert got up and dug his hands into his pockets, like a man searching for small change. "So yuh interested in di job, Christine?"

She thought briefly. "Mi wi come, yes. Mi nuh have nut'n else ah do now anyway."

"So when yuh can start?"

"–Right now!" Matilda said.

"–No!" Christine said, silencing Matilda. "Gi mi yuh numbah. Mi a go t'ink 'bout it and call yuh when mi decide."

"Okay," Albert said, clearly disappointed. He took a card from his wallet and handed it to her. "Wish yuh coulda start today but...think it over nuh."

"Fi yuh head mus' ah tek yuh," Matilda said. "Yuh ah get wuk an yuh deh form fool like yuh nuh know seh wuk hard fi get —"

"— Granny, mind yuh false teeth dem drop out ah yuh mout'," Christine said. "Yuh jus' ah chat so like yuh nyam fowl batty!" She hissed her teeth.

"Christine yuh shouldn't ah talk to yuh granny like that, yuh nuh. Show some respect."

"But she jus chat too much some time!"

"It nuh matter!" Albert said. "Respect her still. She is yuh granny."

My God, she rotten! Albert thought. It would take a whole lot of work to bring her to what he wanted her to be.

As Albert drove back to Kingston, he wondered if he should even bother. Christine was probably comfortable with who she was and wouldn't take kindly to him trying to change her, make her into who he wanted her to be. On the other hand, if he didn't at least try he would never know if it was possible — or worth the effort.

Should I even bother?

If Christine bothered to call, he would bother to try. He would.

Seven

It was now evening. Christine was lying in bed staring at the ceiling. Albert's visit had been over seven hours ago. Since then, she had done little more than think about his offer. She knew she really didn't have much of a choice. No telling when another job might come along. She guessed she could sell a pig or two when the sale was there but how often was that? For the weeks she worked at Eagles, not one pig was sold. And even if she could get them sold she wouldn't have enough to last very long. Seven pigs didn't generate the kind of income one could retire on. She didn't want to sell them too fast now, either, or she might just miss out on a better price later on in the year. It was now March. The season of lent had begun. This meant the prices of pork and most other meats were usually at their lowest and probably wouldn't pick up again till closer to Independence Day in August.

She wasn't quite sure what Albert's motivations were though, and that worried her. He seemed like he really needed someone to work for him but why her? Why did he really come all this way to handpick her? He never saw her work for any length of time so on what basis did he make his decision? Then again, Christine thought, maybe he'd been watching her for the whole four weeks but she just never noticed. If that was the case, he really was the weirdo fuck she thought he might have been when she first saw him.

Shoat had tried to jump her while she was doing room four as he had requested. "T'ink mi wouldn' ketch yuh?" he'd said, grabbing her from behind and slapping her ass. "Gwaan tight with di pussy like it nuh mek fi fuck."

He probably never thought Christine was that strong for when she turned around with some force he was sent stumbling back toward the closed door. Shoat smiled and came at her again. "Yuh strong," he said. This time Christine reached behind her and held onto the first thing her fingers touched. It turned out to be a glass pitcher she had taken in for him from about an hour before. The ice had melted but there was sufficient water in it to almost double its weight. With one swing she let it go in his head, pitcher and all. It hit him hard. The glass shattered, releasing water to the floor like a clear vomit.

"Yuh fuckah yuh!" Christine said.

The blood came now, oozing from Shoat's temple. He fell to his knees and slapped his face in his palms. He fired her right there. "Dyam bitch! Yuh fiah," he said. "Yuh can tek yuh raas an' go back a Macca Tree. Yuh fiah!"

As Christine stepped over him to leave she said, "Kiss mi ass." For this, she was sure Albert never got a good recommendation from Shoat — unless he was the kinky type that liked to be beat up by women. If so, she was here for him if he made the slightest wrong move.

She had to be careful.

It wasn't only in America that you had the crazies. Serial killers and serial rapists were everywhere these days. Sometimes Christine wondered if it was the cable TV that was bringing the idea to so many other persons in other countries. Or was it that seeing it on cable gave them a feeling of validity and so they came out full force?

Her handbag was hanging from a nail on the back of the door. She went for it and pulled out an eight-inch ice pick. Seeing it was there, she put it back and went back to lying down. If that Albert man ever tried anything stupid, she would use it and make sure he never walked again. She didn't consider herself a violent person but she was big on self-preservation. She was done with being knocked around by men who thought they were king cocks. Enough was just fucking enough!

She turned to her side where she felt most comfortable. Both arms were under her pillow, hugging it like a teddy bear. She missed George. In his last letter, he told her he would be calling her this weekend. She would make sure she was home for him. Two years was a long time to be away from the one you loved. She read his letters ten times over and each time, they all seemed like the first reading. Every time they seemed to bring new meaning to their love, like a wonderful poem.

What bothered her most to this day was that she never allowed him to make love to her. She could remember the last time they were together in this very room all too clearly. They were in bed, him on top of her, kissing her lips and fondling her breasts. Then his big hand walked down to her skirt and under it. It felt strange going all the way up her thighs. He was almost in her panties when her hand reached down and quickly grabbed onto his.

"Wha'?" He'd said, frightened but not totally surprised.

"No," Christine said, shaking her head slowly.

"But yuh seh todey, todey yuh ah go gi mi some.. .nuh dat yuh seh?" George tried to keep calm and not shout. Jodi-Ann was on the other side of the bed, fast asleep. He didn't want to wake her. If he did, the pussy would just go further away from materializing. Christine knew that too so she tried to be calm herself.

"Yeah," she said, "But mi still nuh feel like..." she trailed off and then added, "Yuh can eat it if yuh want though."

"Eat it!" George said. "Yuh t'ink man can jus' git up everyday an' ah nyam pussy, nyam pussy so?" He grabbed the bulge in his pants. "Cockie Boy want some too, yuh nuh."

Christine sighed. He was right. They had been going together for a full eight months at that time and they never did it once. Cockie Boy was starving for her. Sometimes, she really felt like she wanted to give him some but when he touched her or when she thought too much about it, the feeling would vanish and then she would start feeling nauseous. She would start remembering the awful feeling of having an uninvited man inside her. It made her feel nasty and dirty all over and when George touched her she was always brought back to that nasty feeling the rapist planted inside her. She was literally scorning herself because someone planted his nasty seed in her. That seed grew into a wonderful little girl for whom she would die a million deaths, but the result didn't relinquish the awful hurt of the act that preceded it.

Christine had pulled the sheet up to her neck and clawed it with both hands. "Sorry," she'd said.

George Taylor was a big man, six three and clearly over two hundred pounds. Added to that, he was a failed boxer. Boxers who didn't quite make it in the ring against a man of equal or better conditioning could still easily flatten a lesser mortal with a single blow. Some of them were always looking to prove this. Some beat up on their women and some beat up on anybody they could get their hands on.

Almost everyone in Macca Tree had a genuine fear of George. Christine knew he could be a dangerous man. But it was that same potential power that had drawn her to him. The first time Christine saw George fight was back in high school. He literally beat the shit out of a boy named William Timble just for stepping on his shoes — and this was just the one instance that she saw. There were also instances where George used his boundless energy and sheer brute force to pummel anyone who happened to cross his path. Word went around that he even beat up his father while he was in early high school but George denied that ever happened. It was his father, though, who suggested he tried out boxing. "Yuh seem fi waan beat the fuck out of everybody so why yuh nuh go mek some money doin' it?" Patrick Taylor had told him in the staff room at school one afternoon. Patrick had been called in to speak to the principal regarding a threat George had made to flatten a math teacher who had dared to hit him in class for not doing his homework. Everybody who heard drew his conclusion from that statement Patrick made that day. Some believed Patrick had only good intentions for his son and wanted to see him amount to something in life. Indeed, boxing was a natural choice for any man built like a bull and loved to fight. Others held the view that Patrick was afraid of George and didn't want another mauling himself so he wanted to get George out of his house as soon as possible.

Whatever the reason, George liked the idea so much that he left school that day and never returned. He went to Kingston the next morning and signed up at the Dragon Gym.

"Wha' you name?" The trainer had asked him. His name was Percival Spencer, a stocky man in his late fifties wearing a washed out Dragon Gym T-shirt and slacks. He also wore a visor marked Dragon.

"George Taylor, sar," he said.

"No man," Percival said, shaking his head and smiling. "Me mean what is yuh boxin' name?"

George thought for a short while. "Mi nuh have none yet, sar..."

'Awright," Percival said, "Yuh is from Macca Tree an' yuh first name is George so yuh name Macca George. Dat cool?"

Macca George. He liked it. "Yes, sar," he said.

He started dreaming about becoming the next heavyweight champion of the world! He could feel the excitement in his bones. In bed at nights, he saw the gleaming championship belt round his waist as he rode the shoulders of his training camp (all of them wearing blazers marked Macca George) after his big fight. He could hear the crowds shouting, "Lick di bwoy unda him raas ribs, Macca George. Kill him blood claat! Jook him, Macca, jook him!" All this made Macca George train harder for he wanted to make it all real. He wanted to lick di bwoy unda him raas ribs. Kill him bloodclaat.

After all.

Percival was not a bad coach. In fact, he was one of Dragon's best. He had been first trainer to a number of boxers who had gone on to gaining some national and international attention. So George was in good hands.

Percival had decided he would be the one to work with George from the moment he saw him walk in through the door. George was tall, lean and quite fearsome to look at. A real prospect, Percival had thought.

In the early parts of training, Percival started noticing his weaknesses but that was expected. No boxer came to the gym perfect. There was always something to be remedied. Lack of right-left symmetry and an unusual predictability stood out as George's main culprits. The symmetry problem was to some degree adjusted but the predictability would remain pathetic no matter how much Percival tried to get George to diversify his moves. This and his slow reaction time (which was discovered when he started sparring with equal opponents and not a shadow) proved fatal to his career.

George got a few amateur fights but failed to spark. It was like everyone he went up against figured him out weeks before and came at him with combination punches, which literally dazzled his slow brain. They always got him in the third round with jaw-breaking uppercuts, sending him to the canvas in an embarrassing sprawl. From the corner of his eye, he was always able to see Percival covering his face and shaking his head. Eventually, Macca George had degenerated to a fourth-rate sparring partner hardly worthy of the lunch he got after each bout. The hype was gone, the dream dead. It seemed the only people he could fight were people who were too afraid to fight him back. Trained boxers weren't afraid. They came at you with all they had. If you gave them the chance, they'd knock your fucking slowpoke ass out of that ring like you were a sack of potatoes.

That was what happened in his last fight. A big, ugly fucker named *Mean Steve Green* punched him so hard, he fell out of the ring and staggered into the stands, raking along a few empty chairs as he went.

He packed up his tote bag and went back to Macca Tree the same day.

George never allowed it to get to him too much though. He considered the failure a natural part of growing up. Sometimes, the dreams you had of a great future doing a particular thing just didn't work out and you just had to accept the limitation and be brave enough to move on to something else. It was never the end of the world.

So he got a job as a bouncer at a nightclub in Old Harbour. That was where he met up with Christine again as she was working as a waitress at the same place. They started dating and got to really like each other. She enjoyed listening to his many stories of trying to make it in the boxing business and how guys like Mean Steve Green (who by then had been making a name for himself) beat the shit out of him.

"Yuh mean like how yuh did beat up Timble?" Christine had asked him.

"Yuh memba dat?" He said, chuckling around the words. It was a fond memory.

"Of course," Christine answered and then added, "Ah fram da time deh mi like yuh..."

"So wha' mek yuh neva tell mi?" George asked.

"Yuh did go weh ah Kingston an' mi did a go have mi baby so mi jus'neva botha," she said.

George never tried to counter this for he knew very well that if he had made it as a heavyweight boxer, a girl like Christine would only see him on HBO. Similarly, if she never had her schooling derailed by the baby, she'd probably be one of those hoity-toity educated jet setters who wouldn't even acknowledge him with a fart. Only now things had evened out a bit. They had both lost a dream and so had to compromise. It was funny how often people got paired up because of this one fucker of a fact.

Their love blossomed over the next eight months but there was no sex. Christine wasn't psychologically up to it and George didn't pressure her. "When yuh ready, baby," he told her, "when yuh ready." George was just so understanding Christine felt bad that she was not feeling ready for him. She tried hard to put herself in that frame of mind. Block out the past and plunge into a new future, she tried to tell herself but it never worked. There was a huge bung in the pipe that circulated her emotions and it wouldn't budge. But she wanted it to, she really did.

This was why when George got the job offer to go to Canada to pick apples she told him that she was going to make herself ready for him. Christine knew George was going to be away for a while and for them to be together like that even once before he left would have been just the right message. It wasn't to be though. She just couldn't.

It was two years now since George had been in Canada and everytime Christine thought of him it made her heart ache because she still couldn't give him what she knew he wanted — even if he walked across the sea to get it right now.

In his letters and whenever he called her, George would always implore her to save it for him. She would say yes but was that really what she was doing? Was she really saving it for him or was she just not giving it to anybody else because she couldn't? The latter felt truer to her for she thought that if she had been having strong sexual desires she would have probably gotten someone on the side to take care of it a long time ago. Two years was a long time to be away from the one you loved. That sort of time could make you do things you wouldn't normally have done. But she wasn't going to do anything and she was glad. Not Shoat nor Albert Bench nor any of those horny boys who walked about Macca Tree looking for new conquests would get her. All she hoped was that when George returned, she would be ready and able to give it all to him.

Christine got out of bed and went to the phone in the small living room. Matilda was in a rocker in the far corner. Jodi was fast asleep in the sofa.

"Yuh ah go call di genkleman?" Matilda asked.

"Yeah," Christine said, "might as well."
"Da's right," Matilda said, "Da's right."

Eight

"Why when yuh go ah work yuh always haffi stay so long?" Jodi-Ann asked from the doorway as Christine carried her suitcases out to the veranda. It was now about four thirty in the morning. Matilda was probably still asleep, Christine thought, for the light was off in her room and Christine didn't hear her stirring to get up. Matilda was never the type to lie around in bed unless she was asleep. Once her eyes opened, she was up and about, maybe unknotting and going through the contents of some black plastic bags she kept her papers in ("So da's if di place flood out dem nuh wet up"). Later on in the morning, she would go out to the kitchen and start a fire to roast breadfruits and make a big pot of coffee.

The fog that slept with the night in Macca Tree still floated above the ground like the ghost of the day before. Soon it would be gone, melted by the rising sun. Right now the only light was that coming from the door Christine had opened and that which came from a rather dull bulb on the veranda.

"Bcause my work different," Christine said. She heard the engine and looked up the dark path. Car lights floated slowly toward the gate like a ship being guided to shore by a lighthouse. Last night, Albert had told her that he'd be picking her up about this time and like a high school leaver on his first job interview, he was here. She wondered if he was always this punctual. Anyway, he did say he wanted to beat the traffic back to town.

"Different how?" Jodi-Ann asked. She now spoke around her thumb.

"My work longer so mi haffi stay dere," Christine said.

"Yuh get more money dan people who go home everyday?"

"No," She smiled.

"Why?"

"Because dem have h'edication," Christine answered.

"So if me get h'edication, me can do likkle bit ah work an get nuff money too?"

"Yes, Jodi."

Jodi-Ann thought for a while. Then she smiled and said, "Me ah go get ah whole heap ah edication den, so me can do likkle bit ah work an' get nuff money so you can stay home."

"Dat soun' good, baby, dat really soun' good."

The engine died and Albert stood by the gate. "Yuh ready?" He said.

Nine

The houses were uncomfortably close together. That was what Christine thought as she heard Albert say, "Welcome to Portmore." At first, she was even thinking that one entire block belonged to one family but then she saw the different gateways and so realised that probably two or three families shared the space. In Macca Tree, some of the homes were very tiny indeed, but they were hardly ever on less than a quarter acre of land. And to think both communities were in St. Catherine yet one was urban and the other so very rural.

The houses also resembled dominoes stacked in little groups. Some people did some amount of painting and "adding on" but quite a number of others were all institution-looking with the original cream colour of the prefabricated walls the building contractors used. Those who did the addition accomplished great feats: some of the dwellings looked like small castles. To Christine, it all seemed so new but not very wonderful. Already, she was missing the space of the countryside. She had worked for a lot of people at a lot of different places but they were all in the more rural parts of Jamaica. She was never much of a city girl and had never sought to know the place very well.

There was nothing but those concrete houses under the hot sun for miles and miles. When she saw the place on TV, she never realised it was this huge. For as far as her eyes could see, there was nothing but yellowish cinderblocks. It looked to her like the dormitory plan of Jewish cities she often saw on TV when there was some war going on. It was funny, Christine thought, that she saw more of those places on TV than she did of Portmore. Maybe it was because hardly anything ever happened in Portmore. Hardly anything worth coming on the news, anyway. Maybe she did see a lot of Portmore in the news but was just not made aware of its expanse. The Jewish cities were often times shown from overhead cameras so you got a better impression of what it looked like. Portmore was also so flat it made her think of the many times she heard on the radio that some of the houses were flooded out due to heavy rainfall. But did it ever rain here? It was just so sweltering now that it didn't seem that way. She had suddenly found herself in a desert.

Albert made a number of right and left turns which looked to Christine like he was always just turning back to the same set of houses on the same street. So to avoid the constant feeling of deja vu she started reading the signs.

WELCOME TO ONE NORTH. WELCOME TO TWO NORTH. WELCOME TO THREE NORTH.

One North, Two North, Three North what a fart! Soun' like prison cell block. Now she was feeling like a prisoner being escorted to her cell. She closed her eyes and locked it all out with the good thoughts: thoughts of going back to Macca Tree for the weekend and talking with George when he called; thoughts of using the money she worked to make sure Jodi-Ann had a good chance of getting a good education (*so me can do likkle bit a work an' get nuff money so you can stay home*) — and not end up like her, travelling the land wiping peoples' floors and washing their clothes.

Albert made another right turn and Christine opened her eyes. The sign on the left now read:

WELCOME TO BRAETON, PHASE TWO
RIDE, DRIVE CAREFULLY
WE LOVE OUR CHILDREN

COACHING CHRISTINE

A mischievous person wrote in yellow chalk just below that: *...And pussy too.*

The turn after that was left into a parking space big enough to accommodate about nine cars. A rust-coloured basketball hoop stood on a tyre rim base at one end like a giant antenna. There was another sign here too. 5 STINGRAY WAY, it said. It was much smaller than the first and was attached to a pole like a Stop sign. About four or five young men were gathered across the way, chatting and laughing. They looked too short for the basketball gear they had on. This was probably all they did, Christine thought, just like the set of idlers she knew in Macca Tree. She guessed there was a set in every town.

"Albert wha' ah gwaan?" A man called from behind one of the concrete fences. The garden hose in his hand was pissing water on the small patch of lawn in front of his small house. Though the question was directed at Albert, the man's eyes and wide grin was fixed on Christine.

"Nuh deh yah, John," Albert replied. He killed the engine and got out.

"Cyaan si yuh at all," John said.

"Well, yuh nuh know how it go, here, there. Taxi man lifestyle..."

"Yeah, yeah," John said.

"Yuh lost sop'm?" Christine asked John as she stood and closed the door behind her. "Yuh jus'ah stare inna mi mornin' soh!"

"Christine!" Albert said. He opened the trunk and took out the suitcase.

"Bwoy, this one yah saucy," John said. "Yuh sista?"

"No," Albert said but didn't volunteer further information. He could roll the case along now for he was on a pavement. Back in Macca Tree the path was stony so he had to lift it to the car.

"Yuh hear seh Snatch get out though," John said.

"Wha' yuh ah seh!" Albert continued walking towards his gate. Christine was right behind him with her bags. Normally, Albert would have stopped to get the news but the suitcase was so damned heavy, even with the wheels working he had to exert himself more than he cared to.

"Yeah man," John said. "Him time up again."

"Him soon gone back in. Is like him nuh tired fi go prison."

"Yuh know it, Albert. Him too damn thief!" John said.

Two grills (a little main gate and a veranda gate), one front door and they were in the living room of Albert's home. The heat came at them from the darkness like they just entered a brick oven. As he flicked the lights on and pushed the curtains aside to open the windows, Christine noticed they too were in grillwork. *You couldn't be too careful*, she thought. Quickly, Albert turned on a big fan that was at the next end of the room. The wind it generated was hot, like one would expect coming out of a sandblast.

Albert opened a door on tne right. "Ah your room this," he said and put the suitcase beside the bed.

"Yuh live alone?" Christine asked.

"Yeah. Mi never tell yuh, nuh? Sorry 'bout that."

Why did he need a helper? Christine thought, as she looked around. For one, the place was not that big. From what she saw, two bedrooms, a living area, small kitchen and a single bathroom for a single man hardly required a live-in helper. Furthermore, everything seemed to be clean and in order. No shirts on the sofa, no socks on the floor and no dust on the bedposts and night tables. Maybe he was just fed up with having to do it all the time.

"Don't let the look of di place fool yuh," Albert said, as if he read her mind. "Mi only clean up because me know yuh comin'. Want to give yuh a clean start. An' besides, mi don't like people comin' to my place an' find it a hog hole."

"Da's true, Missa Albert," Christine said, "for mi go ah some people house fi work a'ready...dutty not ah hog pussy!"

Albert stopped and looked her over carefully. "Now listen to me, yuh see, if you goin' work here all them language have to stay out."

"Yes, sar. But is because yuh seh it mek mi seh it —"

"— I neva seh nutt'n bout nuh hog puss-whatever. I said hog hole. There's a big difference. So yuh jus' cut that out, all right?"

"Yes, Missa Albert," Christine said.

"An' one more thing: Albert is jus' fine by me. Don't bother wid di Missa Albert t'ing. Make me soun' too much like a slave master."

Albert went into the bathroom. He came back in about three minutes. Christine was in the sofa.

"We need to get some lunch now," he said.

"Yes sar. What yuh want mi fi mek?" She got to her feet.

"No, no. Not today," Albert said. "Today we go out to lunch. Relax a little. Talk 'bout yuh future here."

"Mi future?"

"Yeah. Me will tell yuh all about it later."

She felt in her handbag once more to make sure the ice pick was there. It was.

Ten

Albert took Christine to a restaurant called *Lobster Style*. It was at the part of Portmore known to most as the Back Road. Buses and cars used the Back Road when the traffic to Kingston was heavy. It didn't look anything like the rest of Portmore. It was built up on one side with small to medium sized hotels. Behind the hotels was the sea. The other side of the road was mainly swampland. Fishermen also had little huts put up, their boats on the shore like basking crocodiles.

The Back Road was really famous for two main things, though. First, it was the perfect place for cheating couples. The little hotels stretched on for about two miles with more being created constantly, like a baker trying to meet a sudden demand for bread. They operated on an hourly, nightly or daily basis. As a taxi driver, Albert knew that everyone of these places did brisk business most of the time — especially on weekends when he too did great business taking couples to and from their undercover deeds. He didn't agree with their acts but he was not a preacher so he usually just kept his damned mouth shut and collected the money. The only time he had a problem was if they were drunk or if they wanted to get it on in the back seat.

The next thing was its seafood. Almost every hotel offered a wonderful seafood menu. This was what attracted some other people to the Back Road — people who just wanted a good tasting meal they didn't want to (or couldn't) make at home. Albert particularly enjoyed Lobster Style because it offered outdoor dining by the sea.

COACHING CHRISTINE

You could hear the water lapping at the rocks just beneath — like you were actually on a boat. It was one of the medium sized buildings, painted mostly white and had black and white checked floors. He had never had reason to visit one of the rooms but he was almost certain they were just as comfortable as those on the North Coast.

A waiter in black jeans, white long sleeves and a bowtie gave them menus and served water from a steel pitcher. He then quickly left them to think about lunch.

"Ah t'ink I'll have some steam fish an' bammy," Albert said without even glancing at the menu. "wha' you havin'?"

Christine smiled like someone who was really lost but was too embarrassed to say it.

"Yuh can try the shrimp in oyster sauce. It's very good," Albert said.

"Alright," she said.

*****

Christine ate slowly like she scarcely could find an appetite. Albert knew it wasn't that though. Some people just didn't quite know how to eat in public. He was aware that in some of those country kitchens there was a little bench where people would sit and chat while the meal was being prepared. It was also on that bench that they would sit and eat, the plate or bowl sitting in the palm of one hand while they held a fork with the other and dug at the food like a man tilling soil. He could just imagine Christine in Matilda's kitchen, bringing the plate to meet her open mouth as she scooped in some chunks of yam and breadfruit with perhaps a little bit of salt mackerel for flavour. Only she couldn't do that here and so she was feeling out of place. She was like an illiterate woman trying to give the impression that she could read.

Albert finished his meal, sat back and watched her labour as if being forced to eat. She gave up about five minutes later, her meal now looked more like vomit and almost all of it was still there.

Christine smiled and thought, *Fuckin' man nuh stop watch mi!*

"Is what?" Albert asked.

"Nut'n," she said, sighed and looked past him. The people who dined here looked sophisticated. The men were generally considerably older than their female companions. The men also wore wedding bands but the young women didn't. The cars in the parking spaces — except for Albert's Nissan — looked like jewellery on display. Christine could recognise the BMW emblem on no less than two of them. The others, she didn't know but they were equally wonderful to look at.

"Christine, let mi ask yuh a question," Albert said. "You ever meet somebody for di first time an' just t'ink yuh know them all yuh life? Or just t'ink if yuh did meet them before, yuh life woulda better off?"

Christine thought then shook her head. "Nuh really. No," she said. "You?"

Albert shook his head too. "Just askin'. But like how you goin' be with me for most of the week, what yuh husban' goin' seh?"

"Mi nuh have nuh husban'," she said.

"Come on, Christine who yuh t'ink yuh foolin'? Not even a likkle boyfriend?" Albert chuckled. He felt devious trying to garner information in this way.

"Mi have a man yes, but yuh seh husban'. Me an' him nuh married yet."

Yet! Albert noted that word.

"But him nuh deh here," she continued. "Him ah work ah Canada."

Albert stifled a smile. "What yuh sayin' to mi? So him leave a nice, nice girl like you out here by yuhself an' gone Canada? Him mad?"

"Well, him seh him waan fi work so we can have t'ings like everybody else. A apple him ah pick up deh."

"So wha' 'bout when yuh get lonely? How yuh deal wid dat? Nuff man uppa Macca Tree must want a girl like you." As Albert spoke he felt himself getting hard. He wondered if it was the fish that was giving him this afternoon kick in his pants. Making him just want to really ask Christine if she wanted to go upstairs and see what the rooms are like, try out the bed and bath. But he wasn't going to do that. It was too soon. Much too soon.

"Dem want it yes, but da's not all..."

Dem want it. IT!

Albert crossed his legs and folded his arms. "So yuh don't want them too?"

"Me nuh want dem," she said, "me want George. Ah weh him have me want. Everybody else an' weh dem have can stay fi all I care. Me ah save di whole ah it fi George."

Him name George.

"So ah George yuh love?"

"Very much so," she said and smiled.

"How long now him deh ah Canada?"

"Two year, two week and four day."

"An' yuh neva give him bun even one time when the feelin'...ride yuh?"

"Neva," she said. "Yuh nuh hear mi seh ah fi him it?" She smiled again.

"Yuh think him cheat sometime when him over there in cold, cold Canada?"

Christine sighed. "Sometime me t'ink 'bout dat but me nuh mek it badda mi. Him might do it cause ah di distance an all dat. Me can understan' dat."

"Why? Yuh don't t'ink it unfair that him doin' it an' you not doin' it?"

"No. Him is a man. Is so dem stay. Dem can't help it. Dem born fi hunt front."

"Not every man."

"Yuh nuh born fi hunt it?" She asked.

"Well...yes, I guess — but not like that. Ah mean if me hunt one an' get it an' like it, that's the only one me want."

"Dat good fi you," she said. "Maybe yuh jus'nuh love it like how some man love it. Dem nuh jus' love it, dem lub it!"

Lub it! Wow!

"So yuh nuh love it too?"

"Sometime," Christine said. "We can talk 'bout sup'm else now?"

"Sure, sure," Albert said and cleared his throat. She seemed honest in her answers, he thought. It would be wonderful if she really was. She had many rough edges though (Edges she could do a lot better without). He was going to help her get rid of those. He was going to make her into the ideal woman. His ideal woman.

Eleven

Snatch lit up his spliff and took a good pull. He was standing in the parking lot on 5 Stingray Way, with three other men about him like disciples of Jesus. Hengman, Foreigner, and the only one who didn't have a nickname, Omar. Snatch was far from being Jesus, though. He had been in and out of prison more times than he cared to tell. Not that he was ashamed of his record in any way. It was more that he thought it beneath him to brag about the obvious. After all, he was a don, at least to these guys, and not a rass pansy-tell-all.

He did tell them stories of his last stay in prison though. As a matter of fact, that was what he was doing now. They stood close hanging on his words like children listening to a good ghost story. None of them had ever been to prison but they all knew it was just a matter of time before they did. They listened attentively. When it happened, they wanted to be sure they knew how to conduct themselves. It was either that or the police bullets. One of these options was almost inevitable for people who broke into houses, broke into shops, broke into women's underwear and took what they were never given.

Snatch was among the best at this and he had been caught so they knew they should not feel they would never be.

"Ah usually some simple mistake mek dem ketch yuh, my yute," Snatch said and released rain clouds of smoke in the face of the guys. He had just related how the police managed to catch him that last time. He had broken into a house in Greater Portmore to steal electrical appliances but the king size bed looked so wonderfully inviting he thought he might lie down — just for a little while. The owner came home three hours later and saw him there — fast asleep. The police report said he'd even been snoring.

"An' ah waan tell yuh seh," Snatch went on, "Ah not even dat time deh mi wake up neidah, yun nuh!" The men's eyes were peeled as he spoke. It was like a renowned lecturer delivering to a grateful class.

"Eeeh?" Hengman said.

He got his name from hanging dogs people wanted to get rid of. He would take the dog into the hills in one of those large, brown sacks that bulk sugar came in, and hang them from a tree branch like the British did so many of who later became Jamaica's National Heroes. He did it so often till it seemed even the dogs got wind of it and avoided being in his presence. There was one instance where a dog was always shitting in a man named Jerome's yard. One morning, Jerome looked out his window and on seeing the dog stooping to drop his load, ran out clapping and shouting, "Hey dog! Come out ah mi yard. Everyday ah my yard yuh come shit. Ah soon pay Hengman fi bruck yuh rass neck." The dog ran over to his yard, which was just next door, stopped on the lawn and started barking at Jerome. "Arff! Arff! Arff!" The dog was going. It seemed he was actually cussing Jerome, saying: gweh bwoy! Yuh can stop mi from shit? Mi shit any rass weh mi waan shit. Ah dog mi name. Patsy (his owner) tell mi fi shit ova deh cause yuh come een laka toilet. Every damn gal roun' yah sit dung inna yuh face. Wutless. An' Rebecca sit dung deh wid yuh like she nuh know how yuh stay. Nuh mek mi bus' out yuh secret yah bwoy. T'ink mi neva si yuh ova di whorin' gal Suzie last night wid yuh head unda har frock? Every man roun' yah push dem hood inna Suzie. All me too...an' me ah dog, so yuh mus know how it bad. Still yuh gone push up yuh tongue unda har. Damn wutless! T'ink mi neva si yuh, don't it? Don't it?

Jerome picked up a small stone. "Ah soon fling dis an' lick yuh dung…"

"Arf! Arf! Arf!" This could be interpreted as: Seh wha' bwoy? If yuh gwaan talk off yuh mout' mi good as all come over deh an' bite yuh inna yuh rass!

This would have continued but then Hengman came on the street. The dog got a glimpse of him and no sooner, ran to the side of the house and hid itself. No more barking. It was as if dogs could see in Hengman's eyes the souls of every other dog who he had taken away to the Hellshire Hills.

Snatch pulled on his spliff some more and smiled. It was a deep, reflective smile. "No. Is afta di man fi di place go call di police an' dem come wake me up wid di gun mout'. All when mi inna di back ah di cyar ah go ah jail mi ah laugh to mi self."

"So how a man like you mek dat happen, Snatch?" Foreigner asked. He got his name because he was always well dressed. Even now he was wearing a tweed jacket and matching pants while everybody else had on merino and jeans.

Snatch scratched his beard and shook his head. "Dem have a ting weh dem call complacent," he said. "Dat word deh fuck up nuff ah di bes' inna everyt'ing. Mi did jus'start feel seh mi can't get ketch. Even if dem come deh come si mi in dem bed ah sleep, dem woulda jus' wake me up an' me gwaan wid weh mi come fah.

"So how yuh jus'drop asleep soh? Yuh have dropsy?" Foreigner said.

"Is like mi did go ah doctor fi a likkle t'ing an' him gi mi some pill fi tek. Mi neva know seh dem woulda mek mi sleepy. Him did seh it woulda mek mi a likkle drowsy but mi neva know seh ah so dem woulda knock mi out. Mi seh, bloodclaat, my yute, I frighten when mi wake up an si di big gun mout' inna mi face. Den mi si di man dem inna blue surroun' mi like some scorpion, ready fi sting."

"But dem nuh seh lawyer can get yuh out ah dem t'ing deh?" Omar asked.

"So dem seh. But dat deh likkle fart one weh me end up wid neva know one fuck. Den again, mi did have di bag wid everyt'ing mi did tek right beside me inna di bed well hug up." He paused. "One piece ah laughin' inna di court house when di case ah gwaan! Di judge have fi ah lick di hamma pon di desk fi quiet dem dung."

"Wha' yuh seh, Snatch, di court house tun joke house?"

"To rass!" Snatch smiled, pulled phlegm from his sinuses and spat it aside. "When di judge a pass di sentance him seh" – Snatch cleared his throat – "Missa Randolph Gilbert, um, um, yuh come to di court too often now. Yuh deserve nut'n but di maximum sentence! An' him lick di des' wid di blood claat hamma so hard mi ears ring."

"Randolph Gilbert! Ah dat yuh name, Snatch?" Omar asked and everybody – including Snatch – laughed.

Snatch nodded. "Yuh fi hear di middle name..."

"Ah wha' dat?" Hengman said.

"Killcunta," Snatch said.

"Bomboclaat!" Foreigner, Hengman and Omar all said at approximately the same time.

"Ah wha dat?" Omar asked, "African?"

Snatch said, "Afta mi nuh know. Mi parents gi mi so mi have it."

Snatch became reflective for a while, his smile gone. "Mi nuh waan go back a jail again. T'ings change from di early days, yuh nuh," he said.

"Wha' yuh mean change?" Hengman asked.

"Di way di place run, my yute," he said. "Is like di ...administration get different. Certain t'ings weh neva use to gwaan look like a regular t'ing now. Different, man." He looked across the way. A car was just pulling into the parking lot. He shook his head. "Different, different," he said.

Albert and Christine got out of the car. They were all looking at Christine.

"Gal deh sexy, eeh?" Foreigner said.

"Yuh know it," Omar said. "Yuh si how when she walk she ah flash di batty? Have fi good fi manage dem deh, yuh nuh!"

"Nuh mus'," Hengman said. "Some ah dem gal deh weh look like dem can bruk yuh hood root, if yuh ketch dem an' gi dem it di right way yuh hear how dem bawl dung di place."

"Ah true, man," Foreigner said.

Christine and Albert went into the house, Albert lagging behind so he could padlock the grill. As he did this, he looked out and saw them but said nothing. Then he too went in and closed the door.

"Mi know har," Snatch said after a while.

"Eeeh?" Hengman said.

Snatch seemed deep in thought as he spoke. "What a rass," he said, "Christine finally come ah town."

Twelve

Albert knew that if he wanted to have Christine for himself he first needed to get that damned George out of her mind. He needed to make her feel that George was nothing but the past. He would convince her to look toward her future: him. Someone who wasn't going to just fly away to Canada or any other place for God knew how long and leave her to...endure. She said she could wait and it wasn't such a big deal but Albert wasn't going to just swallow all that like vitamin pills. He believed that even if she didn't need the sex, she did need the companionship. She was a young woman and shouldn't waste her life away on some man who wasn't even around. It was like waiting on a parole officer to say you're now free to go anywhere you wanted. If he didn't say it, you shouldn't go. Till then, you were bound to confinement while he lived as he liked. But what made Christine's sentence even more pathetic was that she loved that damned man.

"What if him not interested in you anymore?" Albert asked. He sat and dropped the keys on the end table beside the sofa.

Though they hadn't mentioned it since leaving Lobster Style, Christine knew exactly who he was talking about. "Him seh him still want mi," she said. She went to her room but left the door wide open so she could hear Albert speak.

He came to the door and leaned against the frame. He saw she had a picture of Jodi-Ann on the dresser. She had another picture in her hand, looking at it as if for the first time. Albert deduced the man in it, holding her from behind around the waist, was George himself. He looked tall and ox-strong.

"Yeah," Albert said, "but what if him just sayin' that? What if him deciding not to come back here? Him might have somebody up there who want him to stay with her, yuh nuh."

"Yuh t'ink him woulda do sop'm like dat to mi?"

"Maybe," he said. "You know how some man can be. Especially those who love hunt front. Cyaan satisfy!"

"George love mi. Even if him go out deh an' get dat him still love mi. Cause mi neva gi him none yet an' him still want mi fi him wife."

Albert was shocked by the confession and it showed. He really wasn't expecting to be told so much this quickly. "Never? Not even one time?"

"Neva," Christine said and shook her head. "Not even a likkle chenks."

"Why? Him not up to it?" Albert was hopeful.

Christine smiled. "Him very much up to it. Is jus' me. Mi want to wait till mi married first. An' is ongle three year now mi an' him deh. Him mus' can wait some more."

Albert brought his hand to his mouth as if it were an oxygen mask. "My God," he said. "People like you still exist?"

"Very much so," she said. She replaced the picture on the dresser.

He wondered though, if he should really believe all she was telling him. He couldn't detect any reason not to but you just never knew. Everything she said now just seemed to fall in place with all else she'd told him from the start. *Maybe she's just very good at telling lies.* He guessed that was always a possibility. Women could just throw a lie at you whenever they felt it necessary. They did it with such ease and grace that you had to just believe every word of it. Princess made him realise this. When men lied, women only seemed to buy it just to avoid unnecessary arguments — either that or they had no evidence to prove otherwise. It was never because they actually believed them. Women never actually believed men. They just accepted what they said as workable explanations for their actions. But somewhere in the recesses of their minds, they also knew they could expect to hear some other side of the story at some other point. When women told lies, they covered them so carefully you had to be more than commended if you ever found a truer version of what they said. He never did find out about Princess' lies until he accidentally stumbled onto the truth. It was possible Christine wasn't being totally straight. He had to be careful. Once bitten, twice shy, the sayin' go. *If mi get bite again, mi mus' be a damn ass!*

Thirteen

He didn't know a whole lot about dining out but what Albert knew was still a lot more than Christine seemed to. That was why for the first week of her being there, he took her out to either lunch or dinner everyday. He sometimes got invited to places and wanted her to go along with him. However, he didn't want to set himself up for an embarrassing event. So to make sure she was able, he taught her himself. He was out of a corporate job now but applications were still going out and one day, he believed, he would land another. When he did land that opportunity, it would take him out of the taxi business and earn him a few notches back up the social ladder. He wanted to know Christine was able to climb with him – hopefully not as the help but as a more substantial partner. The things he couldn't teach her, he would have her learn in courses around town.

Yuh have big plans fi her, he thought, *ah hope she nuh do yuh Like Princess...*

He hoped not.

He'd been made redundant from a senior bank clerk post just a month or so before Princess left him. This timing only made the pressure greater. It made him hate a decision he'd made to put his education on hold. After high school at Dinthill, he'd thought of going on to university to become an accountant. So he did his Advanced Level exams and was offered a place at the University of the West Indies. Then he met Princess and all his desires became her — this woman with the captivating brown eyes and Christian principles (she went to church every Sunday and read the Bible every morning before work). Albert remembered, one day, he used the word damn and Princess was quick to say. "Don't use those dirty words. ..yuh must try an' keep your language clean."

"But da — mi mean — that word is not really a bad word. Everybody use' it," Albert had said.

"Not everybody," Princess was quick to tell him. "Not me."

So whenever Albert spoke to her, he tried not to use that word. He always thought he was a principled man; always trying to not use profane language, but here was a woman who didn't even say damn. This was something he knew he wouldn't be seeing very often. It was like God made her for him. Albert was overjoyed.

He fell so deeply in love with his Princess, he could only think of her happiness. All his money, all his time went into her and what they had together. They had many wonderful times. He took her to all the nice places he could afford (and to some he really couldn't but he took the strain and did it anyway). In their second year, he took her on a trip to Cuba and two years after that they were playing the casinos in Aruba. Back home, they watched the sunset in Negril, enjoyed all-inclusive hotels in Ocho Rios and chowed down on jerked pork in Portland. Everyday was like the first day of a child's summer holidays. He enjoyed going out to work too for he knew that it afforded him the luxury of doing so many things with the woman he loved. They had twelve years of nothing but wonderful times. But when it crashed, it crashed hard and Albert was caught totally offguard.

The plan was to get married and have children. They would send them to college and not meddle in their lives like some parents did — at least that was what Albert wanted for them. He could have sworn Princess once had those dreams too but it seemed it quite likely had been a delusion of his.

"Havin' kids might spoil my shape," she'd told him after he suggested it. She was perched on the bed polishing her toenails. Albert was standing by the door just watching her, his eyes fast on the mound between her legs. She was naked. She looked like a cat, tending her paws. God, she was beautiful.

"So yuh don't expect to have any at all?" Albert asked.

"Yeah," she said, "but not right now. Late twenties."

"You are twenty seven, Princess, how much later is late twenties?"

"Next two years, perhaps."

"All right," he said, "So wha' 'bout gettin' married then? Late twenties too?"

"Think we should take our time an' know each other some more," Princess said, "Marriage is not somethin' you jus'jump into like that. That's why so much people gettin' divorce."

Albert should have looked deeper into those words but he never did. He thought she was right. They really didn't need to rush into anything. They had time. She wanted to enjoy her body as a young, childless woman some more. There was nothing wrong with that. If he were a woman, he'd probably want to have all the time in the world before children too. After kids, things got a little complicated. Money you'd use to get clothes had to go into visits to the paediatrician and day care centre. And children who didn't know how to fall asleep would take away those nights out dining or at the movies. Albert could clearly see where what she said made perfect sense.

Not long after the conversation, Princess requested a transfer to another branch.

"I don't think it right for both of us to be working at the same branch like this. We need space to let the relationship grow in a healthy way."

"But don't I give yuh space?" Albert said.

"Yes you do, darlin', an' I'm not complainin'. But because we work together we have to come home together everyday. We live together so we see each other every evenin', every night and in the morning before we leave for work. An' then at work we still together."

"...So what's wrong with that?" Albert asked.

"Jesus Christ, Albert, it's just too much!" She said. "I don't know what to say to you anymore because I feel like it's all been said. We need space to refill our lives with things we don't do together. That way I can have somethin' new to tell you an' you can have something new to tell me. Don't you get it?"

He got it. That too, was perfectly reasonable. It seemed she had given it much thought too for she was able to argue it so very well. They weren't being pressured at work to break up or work at different places ("Company rules, we don't make them, we just make sure they're clearly understood") but he guessed they really needed space to grow. See different things. Albert really had no problem with them both seeing things at the same time but that was just him. He always thought they had things to talk about but that was just him, too. Maybe he was being a little overbearing and selfish. Give the woman some space. It was him not her. Not his Princess. She was right. She always was.

So Princess transferred to the branch at the University of the West Indies and put in an application to start a part-time degree in accounting. The very programme he had given up just to have more time with her. But Albert understood. After all, a woman needed to educate herself.

Part-time studies meant that Princess didn't come home till late most evenings. "Classes are from five thirty to nine," she was always reminding him, "An' then there is the traffic from Mona to here. Lord knows it's not good. It's a good thing Jason live over here so I at least have some company comin' over."

"Jason?" Albert asked.

"Oh I never tell you 'bout Jason? My co-worker...we do some classes together but he's a management major." Then she smiled. "Nerdy birdie Jason."

At about eight fifteen one evening, Albert was at a place called *Moments In Time*. It was a motel along the Back Road, just a few metres from Lobster Style. He had gone there to drop off a man and a woman. The building was all on one level but was long like a dorm with little private rooms. The doors to the rooms were all along the length of the building like shops in a mall. As he pulled up to the door where his clients would be spending their moments, he heard women moaning and groaning as bed heads clapped hard against the thin walls. But one voice stood out in his mind. So as the man and woman went into their room, Albert killed the engine and listened more attentively. It really sounded like his Princess but it couldn't be. *Princess should be in a lecture now*, he thought. *An' besides, Princess nuh use dem word deh.*

"Oh God yes! Fuck me! Fuck out mi pussy!"

"Ah who fah own?" The man's voice now shouted.

"Ah your own," she said. "Fuck out mi bloodclaat!"

Albert felt his heart begin to race uncontrollably for the voice truly sounded like Princess. *But ah cyaan she...*

His head started hurting. The voice was too close. He had to see for himself that it wasn't her. So Albert parked the car across the stony yard and waited there in the dark.

A half hour later, Princess emerged from the room with a man. She was laughing at some joke he was telling her. At one point Albert heard her say, "Him can't manage it." The man chuckled. "Him too fenke, fenke," she said.

"Ah him name Jason," Albert said and they both looked around and saw him.

"Ah she gi' mi!" Jason said and ran off, obviously frightened out of his macho nerves.

Albert remained calm. He didn't have a choice. He could even feel the car key cutting into his palm as his fist got tighter and tighter. He could hear tyres spitting gravel as Jason the 'co-worker' hurried away.

"Why Princess?" he asked.
"Sorry," she'd said.
Albert found it in him to follow Jason's lead.

*****

He'd decided after that he wouldn't be getting so deep with any woman ever again. He was going to become love 'em an' leave 'em Albert. A major playboy. Only his first go at that turned out to be a major embarrassment. When he got the girl in his bed, his playboy machine was more like a plaything that couldn't start. A toy truck as opposed to one you could really and truly get a few revs out of. This was what made him go see a doctor. He did some sessions with a shrink and got some pills. They helped him and he was functional once more but the desire to love or play was gone. He was able to do any damned thing he wanted to but he just didn't feel like doing anything.

At least, not until the day he saw Christine. And now he was in it again. Questions that came to him many times this past week were: what if Christine was just another Princess? How far would he need to go this time to ease the pain?

*****

George telephoned Christine that weekend when she went to Macca Tree. She told him all about her new job.

"So wha' him ah do wid helpa an' is him one live?" George asked.

"Him seh him just want somebody fi cook and keep di place clean fi him," Christine said.

"Den wha' mek him nuh go look a woman?"

"Mi nuh know."

"Dat soun' fishy yuh nuh, Christine. Ah hope ah nuh deh yuh an' him deh an' yuh ah try fool mi up."

"No man, George, ah wouldn't do dat. Mi ah save it fi yuh, baby."

"Yuh better."

Fourteen

Three weeks passed. Albert was now thinking it was time to give Christine another test. Over the time, he'd given her little ones to see how well she could cook, clean and generally take care of his things. She did quite well but that wasn't really surprising for she had much experience as a helper. Her cooking, he thought, was sound in basic principles but she needed a bit more variety to what she prepared. The staples of yam, breadfruit, dumpling and chicken may work like a dream every damned day in Macca Tree, but for Albert it was like hearing a wonderful song too many times. So for the cooking, he had her sign up for Saturday classes at a place called Wilson's Catering Services where they ran short cooking courses. He dropped her off and picked her up himself even though she could easily get a bus or taxi just outside Wilson's main entrance.

"Mi can take di bus, yuh nuh," She told him one morning as he dropped her off. "Yuh nuh have fi come all di way from Kingston to come pick mi up an' carry mi home. If the sun neva so hot mi could even walk cause is not dat far."

He didn't like the sound of that. It sounded a bit too... Princessish! Too much like what she really wanted to do was be out of his sight so she could find some other man. Maybe even have them offer her a lift home. Then God knows what else they would offer her and, like a lift home, she might just take everything else that came with the package.

"Is alright," Albert had told her, "Mi nuh mind comin' back for yuh."

She said she loved the old fart named George and wasn't going to leave him. But the same way Albert was thinking of taking her mind off George, so could some other Joe. If given the chance, that other Joe might just succeed. Albert wasn't going to just sit around and let that happen. It was this thought that brought him to the present test.

Albert Bench drove slowly into the parking lot on 5 Stingray Way and killed the engine. He was parked on the blind side of a removal truck so as not to be seen by anyone on his block. Normally, Albert would have thought a truck parked blocking the view of his home like this a total nuisance but right now it was perfectly fine. It served his purpose well.

He got out of the car and walked sideways like a crab to John's gate.

"John," he said as if he were trying to whisper and shout at the same time. John Cummings was the only person Albert knew he could trust with a test of this nature. He had known John almost forever as they grew up in the same tenement yard on Victoria Street in Down Town Kingston. In those places, even if they were not blood relatives, children had a way of bonding as if they were one big family. Albert, John, Derrick, John's sister Carmen and another girl Albert remembered to this very day only as Boogu Nose. Boogu Nose was always picking yellow-green gunk from her nostrils and showing it to them. Then she would just plop it in her mouth and suck it off like it was custard pudding. She would laugh and they would all go, 'Laaawwd! Nasty!' They played marbles, jax and dolly house in the dirt behind the house, made mud pudding, fought each other, laughed like they were having a fit when the seat of your pants broke, you laughed when you farted and they all ran like they heard a bomb was going to explode. And they shared lunch without making their parents know. Adults didn't like when you shared your lunch. They thought you should eat it in peace so they called you inside and put you to sit at the table. When you couldn't eat it all, they remarked how you were refusing food in a world where so many were going hungry. Then when they turned their backs, you went out to the back of the house and shared the food with the others. Sharing made it taste so much better.

The adults used to see it differently though. They were for the most part hypocrites. They laughed with one another out on the porch and when they met in the yard but behind closed doors they were vile. When Albert was about eleven, his family moved house and went to live in May Pen, Clarendon and so he'd lost contact with John for a couple of years. At the time, he didn't want to move away from his friends but in another way he thought it was good for he wouldn't become an adult there and end up backstabbing his friends the way the other adults did.

They ran into each other again many years later at the National Housing Trust and by some stroke of luck ended up getting flats not only on the same block but side by side. They were adults now so they didn't play jax or dolly house anymore. But then they didn't backstab each other either. At least, Albert knew he didn't and he could only hope John wouldn't.

His brother Derrick was the other option but Derrick was on a business engagement in Florida. He wouldn't be back till the weekend. Albert didn't think he could wait that long. The time for the test was right now.

"John!" He called again. He had to be home, Albert thought. He was always home except when he was working and work was in the kitchen of a cruise ship — sometimes he was gone for months and then he was home for months. He was gone more than he was home though. Dionne, John's wife couldn't stand it. "Bwoy, Albert," John had said one day while they sat out by the parking lot having Red Stripe, "Dionne nuh stop mek up har face everytime mi have fi go weh but mi cyaan help it. Ah jus' di works. Mi try fi get a work inna di hotel dem but nutt'n naah gwaan."

The curtains in the window parted and John's face appeared. *Thank God*, Albert thought. The door then opened. "What ah gwaan?"

"Shh!" Albert went and slipped inside. He quickly closed the door behind him. "Mi want yuh do a thing fi mi," he said.

"Wha' dat?" John asked, intrigued by the hush-hush.

"Me want yuh to call over my place an' jus'chat up Christine for a while," Albert said. "Check her out...yuh know."

"Wha' yuh mean?"

"Talk to her like you want a little fling. Mi jus' want to hear how she react to a man comin' on to her like dat." He grinned. "Jus' a likkle security check."

"You alright Albert?" John asked. He was serious. "Yuh really think that necessary?"

"Yes," he said, He was adamant, like a mad man trying to kiss his own backside. "While you talk to her me will jus' listen on the other line."

"An' yuh sure yuh want me fi do this?"

"Yes, man," Albert said.

"But what if she t'ink me serious an all tell my wife seh me ah look her? How yuh goin' deal wid dat?"

"Don't worry 'bout that," Albert said. "Is jus'ah test me ah give her so when it done me goin' to tell her that."

John fell silent as he thought. "Alright," he said.

Albert smiled.

John went into the bedroom and dialled the number from memory while Albert took up the extension in the living room. They could see each other for the bedroom door was left open. Albert sat in the sofa in an uneasy fashion as if he had a gas problem and was just waiting to get a big belch out.

The phone rang five times and then the voice mail chipped in.

John hung up. Albert hung up as well and then indicated they should try again. John pressed redial and waited.

"Hello!" Christine said. Albert nodded and sat back. He used fingers and thumb to simulate a chatting mouth.

John picked up on it and cleared his throat. It was not that he didn't have anything to say to a woman like Christine. During his days as a bachelor, this would have been another wonderful opportunity to flex his muscles. But since Dionne, he had lost the desire to do that sort of thing. His eyes were focused only on her and his mind taken up with what he could do to make her happy. These days he only looked at girls like Christine. He didn't say much to them for, though he didn't want to brag about it, he knew too well how serious some of them could get even if his intention was to make a compliment and move on.

With Albert listening in, he also felt a little uncomfortable. It was like someone asking you to fuck his wife while he looked on with a shotgun in his hands. "Havin' fun aren't ya?" he might say and when you say no he would say, "Well ya should be, she's a nice piece ah cunt."

"Hellooo?" Christine said after a while of waiting.

"...Um-hi, Christine," he said, "It's me, John."

"...Jahn?"

"Yes, from next door? The short, big head bwoy weh did ah stare pon yuh when yuh jus' come?"

"Oh," she said. There was a brief silence, then she added, "Albert not here, yuh nuh."

"That alright, is not him me waan talk to, is you." He glanced at Albert, just to make sure they were still both seeing eye to eye on the plan. Albert smiled and gave him the thumb to go on.

"Yuh waan talk to mi? 'Bout wha'?"

"About us getting together some time for lunch or jus' a drink. Ah mean, mi deh home most days fi the next couple of weeks an' Albert lef you here most days too. So we could have some fun. As dem seh: when di cat gone, di rat free fi romp."

"But me is not a rat, sar," Christine said. "Me is a big rass woman an mi nuh play dem game deh so yuh can forget it."

John could see Albert's body relaxing as Christine said these words.

"How yuh ah make it sound so?" John asked. "Is jus' for a likkle drink or a lunch, nut'n more."

"Is alright," she said, "Mi eat a'ready an' me nuh waan nut'n fi drink."

"All right then, skip the drinks an' food...Mi ah beg yuh a fuck!"

"Yuh can't get none."

"Wha' mek?"

"Somebody have it a'ready."

"Who? Albert?"

She hesitated. "Yes," she said.

Albert smiled.

"Albert? But Albert can't manage all ah dat him one. Me sure seh if yuh flash di ass two time good, him drop off flat pon him back. Him wouldn't mind some help from a man who strong enough to mek sure when yuh get done yuh stay done till him ready fi him likkle piece again. Ah woman like you want a good manager, fi manage di property well, pump in new stock an increase share value."

"Wha' yuh seh?"

"Mi seh mi ah beg yuh some pussy," John insisted. "Yuh ah gi mi?"

"Fuck off!" She said.

"Christine don't you hear ah say yuh should not use them words in my house?" Albert chipped in to John's surprise.

"Albert?" Christine asked.

"Same one," he said.

"Mi sorry," she said. "is jus'dat him upset mi —."

"It nuh matter! I seh don't use them words."

Silence.

"Yuh hear me?" Albert shouted at the receiver.

"Yes," she said.

"Good!"

John hung up his line for he realised he was no longer needed.

"Anyway," Albert continued, "You handle the situation well. I was totally impressed with the way yuh deal wid it except that yuh mek him believe me is the man yuh givin' it to. That's a lie an' ah don't like people who work for me tellin' lies but then that's another matter. Keep it up an' you'll be working for me a long time. Okay?"

"Yes," she said.

"Good," Albert said, "good." Then he hung up and went back to work.

*****

He went to see his mother that evening. She was in pain. He thought the doctors had found all of the cancer and had burned it out. Apparently not. He hated seeing her like this and knowing there was just nothing he could do. She had more painkillers than she needed yet none of them seemed to be able to help her either. She was still smiling though. In all her pain, she was still smiling. Albert couldn't help but simply admire her for that.

Fifteen

Christine was beginning to wonder if she could stay here with Albert for much longer. His incessant prying in her life had begun to get to her. It was like he was just watching her every move, waiting for her to fuck up. She tried her best but felt like she was just constantly at her worst. Only days after staging the call with John she caught him sneaking under the window outside as he tried to listen in on her telephone conversation. When she saw him, he got up and smiled, dusting off his knees and palms.

"Is who that yuh talking to?" He asked.

"Hold on," she said to the receiver and handed it to him.

"Hello," he said staring at her.

"Howdy do, missa genkleman," Matilda's voice said. It came through with much energy like she was trying to shout to him from across the Macca Tree hills.

"Hi," he said and handed the phone back to Christine.

After she hung up, he said, "T'ink ah man yuh did a talk to."

"So wha' if ah man mi did ah talk to? Yuh nuh expect mi fi have nuhbody?"

"Yuh have who yuh want but not in my house. Yuh talk to dem when yuh is in Macca Tree." He paused and then added, "Don't get mi wrong, ah know yuh mus' have a likkle frien' but I don't want any trouble at my house. Too much time I hear 'bout people comin' to people house to bruck fight over man an woman affair. I don't want dat to happen here so just don't use my phone to call dem. Alright?"

Because of all this, Christine didn't sleep well at night. But while up, she used the time to write long letters to George and mail them the next day. For the past week, she had written no less than two six-page letters — per night! She could only hope he had the time to read all of them. She didn't expect him to write back all the time for she knew he didn't really take very well to writing things down. He preferred to call on weekends and say what was on his mind. For her, this was enough. As long as he showed he cared by calling, he didn't have to write a word. She wrote because she wanted to, not because she expected him to return the gesture.

Honestly though, George was never the reason she saved herself. It was the same reason he never fully made love to her why she perhaps hadn't done it with anybody else since he'd been gone. She simply didn't feel like it. Well, actually it wasn't simple for she thought this was the most complex part of her existence. The physical urges came on and they were strong but as soon as any man got too close to her it jolted her memory to an experience that tore at her very insides every time she did. She had heard of cases where women became lesbians because some man treated them like shit but Christine didn't think she was a lesbian. She knew she wasn't. What precluded her was a deep feeling of being unclean — so unclean that she didn't want anybody else getting polluted by it.

Albert somehow thought she was so naïve that she wouldn't figure out his moves. He was wrong. She was beginning to think he was so narrow-sighted that he could see her, hear her talk and still believe he could psychologically twist her into being with him.

But she needed the money so she was going to play along. Right now, it was the best thing to do. Apart from his prying and sick ground rules, he wasn't really making any demands on her that she couldn't live with a while longer. So there again, George was being a very lucky man, enjoying the best of both worlds, she thought. When George returned, she would simply leave the job and go be with him. He should be able to support them till she got something she was a bit more comfortable with. At least, Christine hoped he would, for this wasn't the sort of job she intended to hold on to indefinitely. She didn't want it to get to the point where she'd have to clobber Albert the way she'd done Shoat. That, she thought, would be too bad for Albert wasn't really that bad a person, he was just a man who expected perfection all the time — a perfectionist who, she figured, also happened to adore her. Shoat, on the other hand was a fucking pervert who deserved every stitch he got for that gash she gave him.

*****

It was funny sometimes how seeing someone can bring a past experience back to your memory all so clearly and — like smelling a fragrance can sometimes take you way back to a specific moment in time — take you back so completely it was like you were literally uprooted and transplanted in that earlier moment.

Christine had just mailed two of her long letters to George, got some orange juice at the shopping centre and was walking back to get a cab home when she saw the man that brought out the worst in her. She never thought she would ever see him again — but then the world was a small place and Jamaica was just a little dot in it.

It had happened just over seven years ago. Christine was at home getting ready for church. She was late. If her mother had been alive probably that would not have happened for someone would have been there hurrying her along. She would not have been left to go to church on her own. Christine never knew her father. She heard he was a policeman. He lived in Macca Tree for a while, but months after her mother got pregnant, he was transferred to another parish and then he just vanished. No letters, no phone calls. Nothing. It was like he never existed at all. The only male figure that frequented the house was a young man they called Gall Bladda. That was what everybody called him. She didn't know why and she never did get his real name. All Christine knew was that he came by almost every day and did work around the yard that was considered a man's job. Sometimes, Matilda gave him money for his work, sometimes she didn't but he did it anyway. He was generous in that way.

On that Sunday morning that changed her life, Gall Bladda came by as usual. "Matilda?" He called.

"She not here." Christine said. She was in her pink, ham-leg sleeved, lace dress and glossy black shoes with pink socks. She had outgrown this get-up for some time now, but it was still all she had which was worthy of a Sunday morning church service. It made her look a lot younger than the thirteen she was at the time. Her face was a little too shiny from the Vaseline she put on as a moisturiser. Her smile was bright back then and her eyes totally innocent. Maybe this was what Gall Bladda liked in her.

"She nuh deh yah?" Gall Bladda asked from somewhere outside. She could hear him coming closer to the back door of the room she was in. He had a machete in one hand for he was just coming from his weed bush. He went there early in the mornings and came by the house for a bite to eat afterwards. Matilda always left his breakfast. It was as if he lived there but didn't sleep there. He was considered not just a friend of the family but family. Both Christine and Matilda were quite comfortable having him around. Gall Bladda chopped the wood, fetched the water from the gully and killed the pigs. He was very handy to have around and he did it all willingly. So, when he came into the room opposite the one she was in, she thought nothing of it. Like he always did, he went to the table and lifted the cover. He saw some roasted breadfruit and salt mackerel. "Is mine dis?" He asked.

"Yeah," Christine told him.

COACHING CHRISTINE

He took the food and went to sit on the floor by the backdoor. He ate all of it quickly. Christine could hear him breathing hard like a wild boar as he ate. She glanced at the clock on the wall and waited on him to finish eating so she could lock up and leave for church. It wasn't far away. She could hear the pastor on the PA system shouting to the congregation to worship God. After this, the deacon came to the fore singing *I Want to go to Heaven and Rest* as the offering was collected. Christine waited.

Gall Bladda seemed to be taking longer than usual. Maybe it was because she was already late why it seemed that way. But he was late too, for normally he would have come by while they were still eating. Today, he was about one hour late. This was not really a problem for her though; she really didn't feel much like going to church anyway. The later she got there, the closer it would be to the end.

Christine was always a little late for church and Gall Bladda knew this. He always left when she was ready to leave, as if he waited around to make sure she was safe and secure. After eating, he would sit under a mango tree in the back yard and smoke weed till his eyes got hazy.

Today, though, he didn't smoke any weed — at least none that Christine noticed. He just sat by the backdoor, looking in but saying nothing. Christine was seeing him through the mirror on the dresser but she wasn't really watching him. Why should she? He was practically family. She could feel him watching her though — just like she sometimes felt Albert watching her when she was in the house. Only now, she was prepared for Albert. She was never prepared for Gall Bladda.

It was getting so late now and she started to feel guilty. She was just going to come and ask him to hurry up when he got up and quickly met her at the door. Christine was somewhat frightened for he had never imposed upon her like this before. He was so close she could smell the food on his breath. The machete in his strong hand made her feel threatened. He held it the way he always held it but this time his eyes, peering at her, made the feeling of impending danger well inside her. He looked like he was getting ready to use it. *Him ah go kill mi!* She thought. *Di weed mad him an' him ah gwine kill mi!* Christine started trembling.

"Go back in deh!" Gall Bladda told her in a low commanding tone that she saw more than heard.

She was about to tell him she was on her way to church and she was very late. He never allowed it though, for before Christine could, he used his right hand to push her back in the room. Frightened, Christine buckled to the floor. She tried to get up but he was on her too soon. She tried to scream but his hand, big and rough, was taped over her mouth. She bit down on it but he didn't even flinch. Her teeth felt like they would break before his crusty palm would hurt. Christine was just about to wonder what he was going to do to her when she felt his hardness penetrating her, rough and fast. The pain was great, she couldn't scream but really wanted to, and the fright of it all was making behind her eyes very hot. For many years, the embarrassment would depress her. After he was finished, he got up, stepped over her and went on his way like nothing happened.

"Wha' happen to yuh?" Matilda asked as she came home later that day. She was furious. There was hardly anything worse than not turning up for church on Sunday.

"Feel sick, granny," Christine said. She was still dressed and in bed. "Sick, sick." She didn't offer more at the time for she wasn't sure what to say. Did the fact that he did that to her mean it was her fault? She didn't know. She felt like it was but then again maybe it wasn't. Was this how it was supposed to be? She didn't know this, either. All she knew was that she was hurting and felt really dirty. As soon as she could get up, Christine had a bath — and then another and another, scrubbing her skin till it peeled. She thought it would make her feel better. Cleaner. It didn't. His weedy scent, his pungent perspiration and the rank of his fluid were still filling her nostrils like he was still there, inside her. It all made her feel so bad, she promised herself she would just block it out of her mind and tell it to no one. Ever.

She saw Gall Bladda almost everyday after that for he still came by the house and chopped the wood and fetched the water as usual. He never said anything about it. It was like she had dreamt it all. Sometimes she really thought she had. She hoped so.

She started feeling really sick. Not the sort of sick she felt after he took her. It was deeper, affecting her insides in a strange way — like she had taken a ride on a galloping donkey and had come off giddy. The feeling wouldn't go away. She threw up a lot and felt generally nauseous. Sometimes, at school, she had to skip classes and go rest in the sick bay.

Mrs. Cray, her form teacher, figured it out first. She had her see the nurse who referred her to see the school doctor for the official word. Christine was by now three months pregnant. When Matilda heard, she just exploded.

"Hafta mi bruck mi back wuk di tuff grung fi sen' yuh go ah school yuh tek it dash back inna mi face!" She didn't want to hear any of it. Christine tried to tell her she was raped by Gall Bladda. She was out of options. Matilda didn't believe a word. Gall Bladda was too nice a young man to do such a thing.

Matilda said, "Mi know him fram him ah likkle, likkle pickney an' him woulda neva do a t'ing like dat, So stap tell lie pon di bwoy before a chap yuh pon yuh mout' wid dah cup yah."

"Den ah how it happen den, granny?"

"Ah yuh gi him!" Matilda said. "Dyam liad! A yuh tek it gi him if him get none at all, so stap tell lie pon di goodly fella."

Mrs. Gray, the form teacher, came by the house and unsuccessfully tried to convince Matilda that Christine might be telling the truth.

"If she telling di truth mek she nuh go a station go report it?" Matilda asked. "Report it an' mek it go ah court go quash out.

Mek di law deal wid it if ah soh it go. But if ah lie yuh deh tell di Lord God will mek sure deal wid yuh."

Christine never reported the incident. She let Matilda believe what she wanted to. Gall Bladda was just too good a young man to have done something like that.

"Eh, carry this go dung a docta Ffrench," Matilda said and pushed a white envelope in Christine's hand. It was now just over a week since the discovery. "Him ah expect yuh dis mornin'."

Christine knew what the envelope and the visit to Doctor Ffrench were about. She had overheard Matilda and Gertrude Buckley, one of her church sisters, discussing it last night.

"If she keep di belly she cyaan go ah school so ah betta she dash it weh," Sister Gertrude had said.

"Same t'ing mi did ah t'ink," Matilda said, "God will understand."

"Yes, Sister Mattie, him always do."

Christine didn't want that, but to them what she wanted didn't matter. She was thirteen and so wasn't qualified to take a mature decision on the matter. Besides, Matilda (Sister Mattie) was the one breaking her back, tilling the stubborn soil to find the money to send Christine to school and let her eat food. This made Matilda the law.

Christine took the sealed envelope and went straight to school where she handed it to Mrs. Gray. It was her only hope now. When she read the letter, the teacher was visibly disturbed. No sooner than she saw it, she took Christine by the hand and walked with her like this out to the car. Soon, they were on their way back to Matilda's.

This time Mrs. Gray was able to convince Matilda otherwise but not without a compromise. The decision was now that Christine would stay out of school, have the child, give it up for adoption and go back to school.

A healthy little Jodi-Ann was born six months later. Matilda was now a changed woman on seeing the child. It was like she was having her first child and the world was singing praises. The child went everywhere Matilda went — even when Christine was not going. She was all smiles now.

For Christine, it was a bittersweet experience for she knew how the child came into being. And because of this she cried day and night for the first month or so. Jodi-Ann's face was so pure and her heart so free of the wickedness that brought her into the world that it created a contrast Christine could not get rid of.

But she loved her baby with all her heart. So much so, that she was certain adoption was out of the question. She wasn't going back to school. She was going to get a job and work and make sure her child got a better deal than she did.

Gall Bladda didn't come by the house anymore. He had just left and nobody could say where he was. Whenever he was around, Christine found herself wishing he were dead.

But today she was realising he was not dead. He was alive and kicking in Portmore like so many others.

"Snatch, yuh ready?" Someone asked. Christine didn't see this person. She didn't see anybody but the man standing just outside the taxi park. The man who turned to the sound of his name being called. As he turned, he saw her. He wasn't Gall Bladda anymore. He had gotten a town name now. Snatch. Christine still saw Gall Bladda though: the man that made it impossible for her to enjoy the sexual pleasures of another man; the man that took her soul and at the same time gave her the person she loved more than the world itself.

"Yeah, man," Snatch said. He looked at her for a while longer before walking off. Snatch turned and looked at her twice as he walked away. He wasn't smiling. He wasn't angry. In fact, the only thing Christine saw in his eyes was nothing. Nothing at all.

Sixteen

Albert had Christine sign up for classes in Mathematics and English. He chose the Pre-University School at Mona because it was in an area where he spent most of his days. The courses were also offered in Portmore but that would be too much out of his sight. Anything could happen. And he knew too well how hot and snappy some of those young college boys could be – he took many of them to and from lectures every day. Better to have her closer so he could monitor her actions by unexpectedly popping up to see her at different times during the day anytime he damned well pleased. After all, it was his money that was going to keep her there.

"Doesn't it make you a little uncomfortable him comin' by here three, four times a day like this? Just to see how you're getting on?" Debbie Sankar, an Indian girl from English class asked one day while they had lunch. Albert didn't like Christine keeping Debbie's company. He thought Debbie dressed too loosely in her batty rider shorts and skimpy spaghetti strap tops. If she wore a button-downed blouse, it was always open at the top, showing cleavage capped by a lace brassiere. Albert thought this was just so unbecoming and he clearly warned Christine against taking up such low habits. The mini skirt never went out of Debbie's wardrobe and neither did red lipstick, nail polish and earrings that resembled compact discs. It was all made worse that she also had her tongue and navel pierced. Her clitoris sported a sleeper too but Albert didn't know this.

"Sometime," Christine told her. "But is not as bad as it look. Him take care ah mi."

"You sound like you're his fuckin' pickney!" Debbie said and bit into a hamburger she had picked up at the Submerge diner. The burgers were good and they were reputed to do wonderful pancakes in the mornings for those who wanted a quick breakfast.

Christine smiled. Her expression told Debbie she had hit the nail right where it made an impression. Albert treated her neither like a helper whom he chose to send to school, nor his woman who happened to be his help. He was really treating her like a child. He wanted to know everything she did during the day and she was expected to sit and relate it all minute by minute like a delayed broadcast of a sporting event. If a man called to her, he expected her to tell him and tell him what she said to the man. Did she get his name? Did she think he was cute or a— (nerdy birdie Jason) — total non-entity? And what about the girls? Were some of them coming on to her like the damned lesbians they were? He knew about them too. He heard them talking all the time when they were in his car. They didn't seem to care who heard them, either. Times surely had changed, he would think. Sometimes he told them to stop talking like that or get out of his car but most times he just let them be. He was beginning to consider it all a learning experience.

"She have a stud in har tongue and har navel for christ's sake!" Albert said about Debbie. "No telling where else she might have one. Damn — (freak) — reprobate! That's most of what the universities putting out these days. So I don't want you getting morally impure by minglin' too much with them. You're there to pass the exams come next June. Some of them just wastin' time an' money because them don't really want to leave. Dem rich man or parents payin' for them so the fact that them have to pay to stay don't bother some of them either. Some taxi man who been workin' that route for over ten years tell me some people who call themselves students been goin there for as long as them been workin'. Maybe even that

Indian girl is one of them. It's just that dem never point her out to me but I can bet she is one."

"She jus'start this year," Christine told him.

"Well you just keep your books in mind cause yuh don't have money to repeat if you fail. Alright?"

"Yes."

*****

Christine did classes at Mona on Mondays, Wednesdays and Fridays. She didn't particularly relish Fridays much for the classes went on till six thirty in the evening. Coming from a district like Macca Tree where many parents didn't even send their children to school on Fridays and from working in the hotel industry where Friday was an all out party day, it was a little difficult adjusting to people treating it like Monday morning. But it was either you did the classes or you missed them and fell behind.

On Saturdays, she had the cooking lessons. Debbie was at those too. In fact, it was here that Christine first saw Debbie but they never actually spoke till they ran into each other at Mona.

"Is follow she followin' you?" Albert asked one day when he came to pick up Christine and was just in time to see Debbie walking off to her wine-red Toyota Camry.

"No," Christine said, "Ah long time now she comin' here."

"That she tell yuh? Liar. I don't trust those lesbian girls, yuh nuh. They'll do anything to get yuh. Be careful."

*****

"I don't care what you think, Christine, but I would leave the bastard," Debbie told her as they walked to class. "Every day he's jus' here, breathin' down your damn neck like a rass vulture. What's his story? Him never have a woman in him life yet?"

"Not really," Christine said, not letting Debbie on to the fact that she was not Albert's woman. The real story would have been harder to explain. "Him jus' protective."

"Protective my ass? You mean obsessed?"

Christine found Debbie good company to be around. She was never boring and had the outlook of a person who had known only the good life since birth. Talking to her gave Christine an escape from the real world. It was the kind of world that you read about in novels. But she was also a virtual stranger who didn't know when to stop talking. Debbie talked about everything — even her colourful sex life — like she was announcing a yard sale. Christine was quite wary and so didn't want to let her in on her life too much. If she said she loved Albert, that was what Debbie would announce to all her other friends who liked to gossip. If this version got out it would hurt less than if she said she was just using him to get an education and as soon as she could manage it, she was going to drop him like he had been flung from a speeding motorbike. Both these stories would hurt George, but George wasn't here, was he? No he wasn't. It wasn't like she was fucking Albert, either. Was it? No it wasn't.

If Albert could only read her mind and see what she was thinking, he would crumple like a ball that has had all its air sucked out, but so what? She didn't give a fuck about Albert and his sick feelings. Christine cared about getting ahead — just like how men so often used women to get ahead. In a way, she felt like she was raping him and it made her feel good. It was just a pity she didn't have it in her to take that cell phone of his and ram it up his ass. That would give her some joy. After what Gall Bladda did to her, she only felt like returning the favour to some of these men who thought they were gods over her. Just like she did Shoat. She deliberately teased him every day she went to work, walking around in those short skirts, knowing very well he was watching her; knowing very well he was going to one day try to force her into giving him some. She knew she would get her chance to rape him back. She did. She was almost certain that one day Albert would also try to get some by force and she would rape him too. After all, who the fuck did they think they were?

Before the pregnancy, she had dreamed of becoming a lawyer. She wanted to be up there in the courts expounding points that would make people look at her and say she was so intelligent, so smart, so beautiful. But Gall Bladda or Snatch or whomever he thought himself to be these days, broke that dream. He was like a bad egg in the world – the kind that spoilt others along the way. When she saw him the other day, she felt like killing the fucker (no pun intended). She still wanted to do it. But she knew that if she did, he would win even more for he had seen most of his better days already and she was still just starting out. Going to prison for his murder would make him win.

She still wanted to get back at him though. Deep down, Christine knew she wouldn't be comfortable with herself until she did. He had done her a terrible wrong – a wrong she spent nights unsuccessfully trying to block out of her mind. It was funny, but she thought the things you tried hardest to forget were so often the ones you couldn't, while the ones you wanted to always remember often times just flew away like feathers in the wind. It was funny.

At length, Christine thought that it was best to leave a man like Gall Bladda to his own devices. In time, she thought, all that he did to her and anybody else would catch up with him. When it did, it would frighten him so much, he would feel all their anguish. No matter where they were, when that happened, they would all feel better.

"At least him love me," Christine said.

"That sounds like the wrong type of love, darlin', the wrong type," Debbie said.

"What type dat?" Christine said. They were entering the class room, now a noisy place as students pulled chairs and desks, preparing for the teacher's imminent arrival.

Debbie dropped her books on a corner desk and found a seat. "The type that make you into a slave. Them days long gone, darlin'. Wake up an' look around you. There are three times more women in this class than men! Dem days are long gone. Be careful."

Seventeen

"Mi see the test grade dem," Albert said. It was now just after five and he was driving home. The traffic in Three Miles was a lot lighter since they had put in the four-way and got rid of that oversized roundabout that made no sense at all. The problem now was the bottleneck just after the four-way as you went on to Marcus Garvey Drive.

She didn't answer. He had gone through her things, Christine thought. The result sheet was in a drawer on the dresser. She kept mainly her undergarments in that drawer and the envelope with the results was kept at the very bottom of everything. She had made sure of that for she didn't want him seeing them. He couldn't have gotten them from the school without a letter from her. Even if he forged her handwriting, they probably would not have given him a copy for she had signed for one just a couple of days ago when they officially came out. It could also be that he had a little sneaky friend in there that would do anything for a little tip every now and then but Christine just didn't think so. He had gone through her things. She would make a special check when she got home. Ask him now and he would probably lie, she thought.

"Why yuh didn't show them to me when yuh get them?" He asked.

"Too low," she said.

"Yuh shame?" Albert asked. "Is your work an' yuh shame ah it. Yuh know wha' dat mean? Yuh know yuh can do betta. But because yuh mek dat dyam waste ah time lesbian gal tek up the whole ah yuh time yuh end up fail the test them."

"Alright man, done," she said, annoyed.

"Seh wha'?"

"Mi seh yuh can stop chat now. Yuh just ah chat so laka yuh nyam fowl batty! Done now man. Cho!"

Albert was silent for a while. He took the right turn at the traffic light by the Tinson Pen Aerodrome and continued toward the Portmore Causeway.

"Ooookay," he said and shook his head. "Is so yuh goin' treat me after I spend my money send you to school so yuh can better yourself? Oookay."

She was now wishing she could take that back. It just came out because she was feeling very pissed at him going through her things like that. Her privacy! Why was he really going through her panties? Was he dressing up when she wasn't there and jacking off in them? She didn't put it past the fucker. Not one bit.

He had a point though. She was ashamed because she knew she could do better. Here was someone paying for her to go to school and she was goofing off like it meant nothing to her. Sitting around all day, listening to who and who got fucked in the bathroom down by the Arts Faculty instead of going to an empty room and getting some work done. She was wasting an opportunity. The price she was paying by putting up with a jerk like Albert meant she should make the most of it. She should really make sure that when this all ended she'd have something to show for it more than high blood pressure.

"Sorry," she said. "Mi neva mean fi seh dat."

"Yuh sorry an' yuh never mean to seh that," Albert said, still nodding. "Ooookay." For the rest of the way they didn't speak.

*****

The phone started ringing at about three the next morning. Albert was not used to getting calls at this ungodly hour and as he fumbled in the darkness to pick up the receiver, he was forced to wonder if it was even remotely possible that the call could be Christine's. Maybe she had had the audacity to give his number to George even after how much he warned her against having any man calling her here.

Albert picked up the receiver. "Hello," he said.

"Yow, Al B.!" The voice on the other end said. It was Derrick. Hearing from Derrick didn't normally give him a low feeling but at this hour it made him feel faint. Like he wanted to lie down even though he was doing just that. Derrick tried to sound unruffled but Albert knew better than to believe he was.

"Wha' happen to mama?" Albert asked, cutting through any intention Derrick might have to lay it on easy. At this hour, there was no bad news that came easy. If you got a call in these small hours and was told that your tire was flat you'd hardly be able to go back to sleep without ruminating on the ills of getting a flat.

"She gone back ah the hospital," Derrick said.

Albert propped up on one elbow. "Yuh serious! When? Which hospital?"

"Not too long ago. Me just comin' back in. She did ah moan because she seh she did ah feel some terrible pain. It get so bad one ah di time dat is like she pass out. To be honest mi did so frighten mi did t'ink she dead. Den mi notice say she still ah breathe. So me an' Gail lift her up an' carry her down to the hospital. Kingston Public. Is like seh di pill dem stop work now..."

"My God," Albert went under his breath.

"Al B., I frighten till I nearly drop dung, too. Is just because Gail deh here an' jump around fast why mi find the energy. When mi see my mama a wrench wid di pain mi feel like mi bowels ah come loose. Serious. Is like de whole ah mi belly did ah go drop out."

COACHING CHRISTINE

"But mi think she did ah get better?" Albert said. "Up to yesterday when I look for her she tell me she was feelin' some pain but the doctors said it will gradually get less till it...gone." Albert felt great sadness that he never picked up on this before. "My God, no."

Derrick sighed. "She fool all of us, Al B., is not just you. Guess we should ah talk to the doctors we'self, but she never seem like she want any help. Guess she just never want us to worry."

"Always protecting us, eh."

"Always."

*****

By 4:15, he was at the Kingston Public Hospital. The roads were so traffic free at this hour of the morning that it made you wish that time would never pass till you were back home. Only you knew this wouldn't be because within another hour everybody would be fighting to get to work.

Albert hated going downtown these days. He thought it was just too violent too often. It was like you always risked being hit by a stray bullet or getting caught in a stabfest. Even when he had clients going downtown, if it wasn't the more sedate and commercial parts like King Street and Ocean Boulevard, he was most reluctant. On North Street, where the Kingston Public Hospital stood, things had a way of getting out of control as suddenly as earthquakes. Over the years, it had become quite usual for persons to enter the hospital premises and harm patients. This was why hospital security had to be stepped up to the point where you had to go through a series of checks like you were going through a US airport.

All this beefing up didn't really make Albert feel any better as there was the other fear he had to face — the fear of hospitals. Now, as he walked to the ward Derrick told him she was in, he felt weak.

He made an effort to avoid the poorly lit corridors for he always thought these were the ones through which orderlies would most likely be rolling out dead people on stretchers like they were coming out with party favours. He didn't want to be seeing any dead people but if it became unavoidable, he would prefer to have the experience in the most well lit place on the premises. So he walked on the outside corridors. It would take him a little longer to get to the ward but the outdoors were more comforting. Besides, Albert wasn't sure where the morgue was and didn't want to just run into it like an old friend you owed money. The shock of that would be like inadvertently stepping into the path of a speeding eighteen-wheeler truck.

He looked across the courtyard and saw Derrick coming toward him. Thank God, Albert thought and made some long strides to his brother.

Derrick looked like he had lost weight. He was never a huge man but at least his jeans never just hooked onto his hips like they did now. Was it possible he could have lost so much weight over one night? This thought made Albert wonder how seeing Ester would impact on him. The fear that left when he saw his brother had now returned with renewed vigour.

"Come," Derrick said and led him to the Edwina East ward.

This was another experience all in itself. Everybody looked really sick. The room was long and lined with single beds. It reminded Albert of sick bays in World War II movies. The smell of some chemical or the other was strong in his nostrils. It smelled like a purple, alcohol rub his grandmother used to keep around her house. She called it spirit and used it to soothe her arthritis. Added to this was the constant hiss of steam being released from something just outside to the back of the building. It was like the sound steam trains made when they were at the station. Albert had no idea what it was and he didn't want to find out.

Visiting hours had not yet started but it seemed on this ward the rule was not strict because they were able to walk right in. Albert couldn't help but think that maybe this was because things were so far gone with these patients that there was no reasonable guarantee of them making it to the official visiting period. He hoped that was not it but his mind kept daring him to guess again if he had any other ideas.

Ester's frail structure made the single bed look more like a double. Albert felt himself sway but he quickly snapped out of it. He couldn't let her see the horror of her illness reflected in his eyes. He had to be strong.

Albert leaned over, hugged her gently and kissed her cheek. He smiled to keep back the tears, "Feel better?" He asked and felt really stupid for doing so.

"Much," she managed. She actually sounded stronger than she appeared. Her eyes were yellow and her skin as taut as rubber. It was like all her muscles contracted to form one mass over her bones like the rubber cushion on the handle of a hammer. The burns from chemotherapy were more evident now that she was wearing only a nightgown with no house robe to hide them. That radiation thing seemed to do more harm than good most times. It all seemed so damned primitive, like they were roasting you alive. He could swear he could smell burnt flesh and, under normal conditions, it would make him sick. But this was not a normal condition. This was his mother.

Ester tried to turn but couldn't. They both helped her. She pointed to the Bible on the bedside table. Albert picked it up. It felt cool in his hands. "What yuh want mi to read?"

"Anything," she said.

He felt like crying again but didn't. Couldn't. She needed them to be strong. As a child, she used to have them read a Psalm every night before they went to bed. Any Psalm. So he opened the book to Psalm 23 and read it for her, for all of them.

Eighteen

"Mi ah go dung tomorrow. Come back Monday," Christine said. She was in the kitchen doing up some chicken soup Albert would be taking to the hospital for Ester. He was in the living room, pacing and shining his shoes. He stopped and looked at her as if she had slapped his face.

Ester's illness was affecting Albert worse than he ever thought it would. Not that he was expecting her to become this ill after all the treatment but as any reasonable man, he did think of the remote possibility and the effect it would have on him. The way he saw it, he would probably feel a little down that it had come to this and would then accept it as a natural part of life. We all got sick at some time. But now that it was actually happening, he wanted it to stop. He felt he had the power to do this and if he didn't, whatever the outcome, it would be his fault. He also believed that his presence at the hospital would help her recover to full health again. Maybe she'd fallen ill to this extent because he didn't go to see her often enough while she was at Derrick's. He used to go there almost everyday and, when he couldn't make it, he called. But now he was thinking he should have gone there two or three times a day. Never just call, always be there. Going downtown didn't seem like much of a risk any more. But all the visits and work he was now putting himself through to make sure he did all he could for her was making him very tired. So much so that he felt fatigued most of the times like he was running an endless race in noonday sun.

COACHING CHRISTINE

Added to all this, Christine was now telling him she would be going to Macca Tree for the weekend. It was a time when he needed her most and Albert would have none of that.

"So why yuh have to up there so long?" Albert asked. "Matilda alright an' Jodi-Ann alright. Is not like one of them sick..."

"But dem nuh have to sick," she said. "Mi jus' miss mi yard an' feel like goin' home."

"So when you gone what yuh expect me to do here alone?"

She handed him a mug with some of the soup. Steam rose from it like transparent snakes. Albert had some. It tasted bland... but it was perfect for Ester. It was what the doctor ordered.

"Not even one day, but three! No, Christine, that too long."

"But is not like ah have anythin' here to do now," she said. "Everyt'ing done do already an' the place jus' hot an' ... borin' ..."

"Borin'?" Albert said, "Yuh learn new word. That good. Keep it up. But what about my fresh made breakfast? What about di little soup me ask yuh to make for mama when ah goin' to look for her? Eh? What about that? That can't be done from today yuh nuh, or it won't be fresh made again." He had some more soup and sat in the sofa. "An' why yuh think yuh have to go this weekend? Why not next weekend? Yuh have something special to do up there this weekend?"

"No," she said, "mi jus' waan go home, da's all."

"Well, yuh can't go," he said.

Christine went silent for a while, very contemplative and apparently subdued. She couldn't believe what she had to go through with this man. It was like she was a prisoner in her job. Sort of like slavery, too, she thought. It was not an entirely new experience, though, for her last employer had made somewhat similar demands on her time. Only Shoat was serious about work and usually had a lot of it to give her when he wasn't trying to get frisky. Albert, on the other hand, didn't have that much here for her to do. As far as she was concerned, she could go home every evening and she would if she didn't live that far away. In fact, most of the time there was no real work to be done. He simply wanted to keep her here for his personal reasons. Christine knew this. I would have been an ass if I didn't pick it up by now. Albert was completely jealous of her. He seemed to be always afraid some other man was going to steal her. Whenever she went home, he feared George would somehow be there waiting for her. And, if he weren't there in person, he would probably give her a call. That was what bothered him, she thought. He didn't want George to even call her. The less she heard of him, the more she would think he had forgotten her and the more wonderful and eligible Albert would begin to seem. She bet Albert would even take the picture of George she had on the night table, and throw it away if he could. She saw the way he looked at it when he came into the room. It was like having a dog at home that you didn't like but tolerated because your wife just adored the ugly little fucker.

"But yuh can't stop me," Christine said.

"Say what?"

"Yuh deaf?" Christine said. "Mi seh mi ah go home an' yuh can't stop mi!" She rose her voice now, so he wouldn't miss a word — couldn't, really.

"So you decide to walk out on yet another job in what, under two months? Great goin', Christine, you'll do yuhself a lot ah good by carryin' on like this. Keep it up."

Christine started for her room. Albert was quick to follow. "So is really that yuh goin' do?" He said.

"Move out ah mi way, man," she said as she made an about turn for the bathroom. As she passed by him, her ass bounced him aside and he had to stagger his feet to stay standing. She slammed the door behind her.

"Christine, wha' 'bout mama soup?" Albert asked, clutching for a reason she would accept. "Yuh know me cyaan cook it nice like you."

"But yuh nuh have to cook it at all," she said from behind the door. "Yuh bredda can cook it or mek him people them cook it. An' if dem nuh waan do it, she can always nyam di hospital food."

"But mi want it fi come from me...is the least I can do now."

"Well cook it yuh fuckin' self!"

Albert sighed and went back to the sofa. "You gone back to them dirty words?" he asked.

The toilet flushed and the tap came on. In another minute, Christine was back in her room and Albert was again behind her.

"Some good discipline is wha' yuh want," he said.

For the first time since returning to the room, Christine looked at him. "Wha' mek yuh nuh come gi mi di discipline? Come gi mi nuh? Come Missa Albert, gi mi di discipline an' mek ah get fi bus' yuh rass head wid dah vase yah."

Albert looked at the vase on the dresser. It looked heavy enough to knock him out cold if she used it. She seemed quite serious too.

"So wha' 'bout the classes? Yuh don't plan to finish them?"

Christine took her bags and put them on the bed. She then started putting things in them. She really liked the education process. Her mind, for the first time in a very long while, felt almost like it did when she was a first former, full of dreams and possibilities. She was getting a real second chance with these classes, one she didn't want to just throw away but the fucking man was getting on her last nerve! *Jus' endure it some more*, she thought as she piled clothes into her bags. *Endure some more an' get wha' yuh can get out ah him. Den yuh can tell him fi go fuck donkey while yuh go start yuh good life wid George.*

But Christine didn't listen to her mind today. This ordeal had gone on for too long now and she was tired of it. She needed out. She wasn't sure what she was going to do after leaving. Another job might not fall in her lap like this one had. But just as she left Shoat (Oh! Oh!) and didn't die for it, she believed she would be able to make it through this one too. Christine picked up the bags and took them out to the taxi stand. Albert ran after her. He didn't have any shoes on.

"Alright, alright," he said, "no need to let it get to this. You can go this weekend. I will take you there and come back for you on Sunday."

Christine kept looking up and down for the first cab. There was none in sight. "Mi not comin' back till Monday," she said.

"Jesus Christ, Monday then," he said. "jus' come back to the house an' get de things ready fi mama for me."

It now seemed her resolve was relenting. She looked at him and shook her head. Albert found it in him to smile.

"Mi nuh know why yuh have fi mek it so hard," she said. "Why yuh can't trust mi enough fi go home an' come back? Yuh t'ink mi have man up deh but mi nuh have none...di one man mi have deh ah Canada."

"But me nuh care bout who yuh waan look for," Albert said. "Mi just want di work done..." He took her bags. She didn't resist. "Come, Christine, just do the things for mi an' mi will carry yuh up there and come back for you Sunday evenin'."

"Monday." She was adamant.

"Alright Monday."

*****

On Sunday, Albert drove up to Macca Tree and checked if she was ready to leave. He could have called but had decided not to. He was hoping that just presenting himself there would make her change her mind. But he knew very well she would say no. She did say no, but he didn't feel bad about making the trip just to hear that for at least he got to see her face. He was finding it hard to go a single day without that these days.

Nineteen

Two can play the game. She was alone in the house as Albert was out at work. She had never looked through his things before but today she thought she would.

It was now two days since she returned from her weekend in Macca Tree. Albert had done something last night that made her wonder why she came back at all. He had gone to pick her up at school and she wasn't there. She had left with Debbie and two other girls for a while to get some brochures on a new cellular phone Debbie was planning to purchase. She never had an interest in the damned thing but Debbie insisted that she came along if just for the fun of it. She did just that. When they got back to the campus, Albert was there waiting. It seemed he had been there a long time for his brow was furrowed and he sat with the car door open, his legs hanging out. A half empty soda bottle stood on the pavement beside his shoes. Wordlessly, Christine got in the car beside him.

"Good afternoon," she said after a long uncomfortable moment of silence.

"Where were you, Christine?" Albert asked in a huff.

"Half-Way-Tree," she said.

"Half-Way-Tree," Albert repeated and nodded. "Is Half-Way Tree school is now?"

Christine didn't answer. He was very early anyway. That's why he had to wait. The time she got back was just about the time he usually picked her up.

"What were you doin' in Half-Way-Tree?" Albert asked. He maintained a forced calm, as if he was really thinking about a million possibilities.

She told him the whole cellular phone story. Albert listened attentively but she could tell he wasn't accepting it. It's as if he knew what was true and was waiting for her to make her web of lies and then catch her in it. Christine told it anyway — it was the only one she knew. As she got to the end, he started the car and drove home.

*****

It was when they got into the house that he held her. She didn't know how to react. She wondered whether he was going to try and rape her. He couldn't be that stupid. She never thought Gall Bladda was going to, either, but back then she was the stupid one. Things were different now. She slept with the ice pick under her pillow every night. She could keep him off long enough to get it if he tried anything stupid. But he wasn't going to and deep down she knew that was not his intention. So even when he pushed her to the sofa and hunched over her, Christine didn't feel threatened.

What he did frightened her nonetheless. Albert brought his face close to her as if he was going to kiss her and started smelling her from head to toe like a dog would — only slower. She sat there looking at him, not sure what to make of the situation.

"What yuh doin'?" Christine asked after a while.

"Checkin' to see if you did have anybody all over you," he said, unperturbed. He stopped at her hands and smelled them again. "I don't have this soap here, how yuh hand smell like some sweet soap so?"

"Because mi wash dem afta mi piss," she told him.

"You must know how to talk to me. I keep telling yuh that."

"An' yuh fi know how fi treat mi. If yuh nuh treat mi right, mi chat to yuh anyway mi feel like."

He got up and stepped away. "Sorry," he said and went to the bathroom. He remained in there for about ten minutes then he came out and left the house.

This was it. She wouldn't go on any further with this. But before she did, she would try to see what kind of man she was really dealing with here. As he left that morning, she gave herself a clear hour then went into his room. She turned off the radio and TV so she could hear every sound — in case he thought of coming back earlier than usual. She felt nervous, like she was going to a strange and dangerous place. She went to his room almost every day, dusting and picking up whatever she thought he would want her to pick up, but today was different. She was going there to do something he would never tell or want her to do. She was going to go through his things just like he'd gone through hers. She saw herself in the dresser mirror as she stooped to open the drawers and had to stop for a moment. She thought she looked quite devious but she knew she wasn't. She was just a girl who wanted to know more — all a part of her education.

The drawers were locked but that was of no serious consequence for those drawers were the very same as those in her room. It was a cheap way to make locks but it seemed cabinet makers didn't care much about unique locks for there was nothing to hide in a dresser or cabinet or wardrobe.

Careful not to disrupt anything, Christine went through the drawers one by one. The first three had nothing that sparked her interest, just clothes and rejection letters from job applications.

The last drawer, however, was a different story altogether.

When she opened it, what she saw totally blew her away. Prozac was but one of the descriptions scribbled on the over one dozen little plastic bottles. They still had pills in them for the most part like he — or somebody — started feeling better. Doctors usually advised against this practice, Christine thought as she dug deeper. There was a black book with Executive Diary 2002 written on the cover. She took it up and started to read. Her palms got sweaty as she realised she was really onto something. She wiped them on her jeans and proceeded.

There was nothing written in the diary from January to March 12. Then the scribbles started on March 13 — the very day Shoat fired her. She remembered. It was the day she saw Albert for the first time, standing on the stairs, watching her. The day he saw her.

She read slowly as the writing was terrible — like whoever wrote it shook profusely — but she could make it out anyway. It made her tremble.

> Princess, I don't know what to do anymore. It is like my life is over, I think it is. I've tried everything and I think every doctor. They all say I'm alright and I'll be fine. But what do they know? Last night, I dreamed about you and that man again just like I saw you two leaving the hotel and laughing at me. It's been every night now. How do I get over this? It's been two months. There is only one way out, I think.
>
> It's funny you know, Princess, but this silk tie is the one you bought me last year as my birthday present. It's now going to become my death day present also. It's funny. I've tried dealing with this another way but nothing works, Princess, nothing works. I still love you though, but you hurt me. You hurt me bad, bad, bad, bad.
>
> I don't want you to think of what I do too much though for you could not save me even if you were staying here. I would do it anyway. You cheated and I could die for it. I think it's a reasonable price to pay to God for breaking down such a wonderful thing he gave to us. I tried to figure out what it is that I did wrong for you to

turn on me like that but I can't seem to figure it out. Do you know the answer, Princess? If you do tell God when you get to where I'm going, for I sure as hell don't have a clue. I gave you all the money I could give, I loved you every day and never hesitated to tell you so, I paid the bills, I never hit you once, I remembered the birthdays, the special days we shared and had good relations with your parents. Your family seemed to like me and when I asked you about the sex, you told me it was the best you've ever had. The best until you found better, I suppose. For so many years it was great and then you just did this to me. How do I recover? Were we together too long? Did I love you too much? Find the answers for yourself for I really don't need to know them anymore. Nothing matters now but to end this terrible world of mine. End the awful, stomach turning pain. I tried. God knows I tried.

Love, Albert.

Christine rifled through the rest of the diary but nothing else was written in it. There was an envelope just beneath the diary that was addressed to Princess Cummings. The envelope had on what looked like enough stamps to mail a small package. He wrote on barely two pages but, it seemed, he was going to send her the whole book.

"Oh God!" Christine said under her breath and sat on the bed. She now had some idea of why he was like this. At least so she thought because he could have been like this and that was why whatever happened did. He was overly present in her life but Christine thought he was a nice man anyway. He didn't deserve this. Everybody has faults, she thought. He worked hard, he came home everyday on time and he wasn't really unkind to her — except when he got jealous. Even at those times, he never cursed her in any degrading way nor did he ever lift a hand to hurt her. Bad things sometimes happened to good people, she thought. You played by the rules and the rules played you by. It was as simple as that.

She wasn't going to leave anymore. One voice was saying all this evidence was why she should but she still felt she wouldn't. She would stay and see if she could probably change his way of thinking and make him know not every woman was like that Princess. The only way to find out was to live your life trying. There was no sure bet that it would never happen to him again nor was there any rule that if he watched her like a hawk, she wouldn't do that to him. She wondered if he would ever come to accept this.

*****

While Christine was thinking what a rough deal he got from Princess, Albert was taking a client to the airport. Her name was Ruth and she was one of his regulars. He drove her to the Mona Campus most mornings of the week. It was unusual for him to be going off to the airport with her. Since picking up Trevor's wife, it was the first he was going back to an airport for any reason at all.

He took Ruth to the Departure section and helped her get her bags inside. The traffic warden just outside was having a fit because he parked by the main entrance. He promised Albert that if he stayed too long he would have a tow truck pull the old car away because, "A so unoo Jamaica people stay...just love bruck rule!"

When a taxi took someone to the airport, they didn't just turn around and leave unless they had urgent business to conduct. They waited around for a while as someone was always in need of a taxi. Albert didn't have to wait very long before he saw a man calling him over. The man had three suitcases on the pavement about him. The cases seemed stuffed and heavy. Two could go in the trunk and the other on the back seat. But there was something else Albert thought as he approached the tall man and picked up the first two cases. He had seen this face before. It was George. He was sure of it. The man looked just like the picture Christine had in her room. But she never did say anything to him about George coming home today. Maybe he wanted to surprise her, Albert thought. But she wasn't in Macca Tree. Maybe he would let Matilda tell him where she was and then he'd come down and give her reason to smile – like a damn prince charming.

Or maybe she know him comin' but just never say anything to me, he also thought. They got in the car and Albert drove out of the airport before asking, "Where to?"

"Old Harbour," he said.

Maybe it wasn't him; just a look alike. No, it was him. Albert saw the Air Jamaica nametag on the suitcase and it said George something. He was sure of that. Coincidence? He didn't think so. The only coincidence was that he ran into him on a one off trip to the airport.

As they got into Old Harbour, Albert remembered what he didn't like about the place: for a small town, it was just too congested most of the times. Leaving Kingston, you would expect to be in a place where your car could move smoothly from street to street, but, in Old Harbour, you had to endure the traffic. The new bypass helped a lot, but mostly if you really didn't have business in the small town.

When he got to the house, a woman and a child came rushing out.

"Daddy cooome!" The child said. The woman stood in the yard till George went over and swept her up in his strong arms. The child hugged onto his long leg. While all this went on, Albert put the suitcases on the veranda and then collected his money.

As he drove back to Kingston he thought, it couldn't be him. It couldn't be him at all, at all. But he knew it was. It was.

Twenty

There was a knocking at the gate. Christine awoke and looked into the light streaming in through the half opened window. Then she looked at the clock. It was about ten past one in the afternoon. She wondered who that was. Albert never told her to expect anyone at this time. If he knew somebody was going to come to see him, he would have stayed home — especially if it was a man. He would never want to know that a man was here with her, waiting on him.

As she got out of the sofa, she vaguely remembered the dream she was having before the knocking pierced her head. She had been dreaming about George. She was missing him so much now she was beginning to wonder if she could last till he got back. Would she just drop dead from missing him? Could she? As for the sex, she sure as hell felt like getting some but it wasn't going to happen. She knew that even if she tried the feeling would leave her as soon as anyone, whoever he was, tried to enter her. If the person was just satisfied with eating her like George did, she would probably take the chance but who else was going to do just that? Albert? She didn't think so. She didn't even think he would want to eat it any at all — even if he was going to get further afterwards. His mouth was so close to it yesterday as he sniffed her all over, she was almost willing to push his head onto it and coax him to lick some for a little bit. *Maybe that would lighten him up a bit,* she thought. *Maybe it would lighten us both up.*

But what would she think of George then? Would she still love him or would she start thinking it wasn't necessary anymore for she now had another man who was willing to lick her till kingdom come without asking for more? She didn't know the answers to these questions but just thinking about Albert's prim and proper mouth rooting between her legs made her wet.

"Who is it?" She asked. She was still sleepy and her voice sounded groggy. She was also thirsty. It was the heat that had put her to sleep like a drug. It made her turn uneasily but unable to wake up effectively. Each time her eyes opened, they fell shut again as if they had bricks tied to them. As she rose and walked toward the door, she felt weak like she could tumble over if a slight wind stirred. The fan was on but it didn't matter. She pulled her jeans skirt around her and zipped it up for she had loosened it while she slept so whatever air there was could get on her bare skin. It didn't work much but the little it did may be what kept her from just fainting, she thought. After dealing with this person, she was going to take a nice long shower. But the water in the pipes wasn't exactly cool so it probably wouldn't make her much cooler.

"Hi, Christine," John the next-door neighbour said as she opened the door. It was almost just as hot out here as inside. John stood at the gate with a big smile on his face. "I was goin' up to the beach an' wonderin' if you interested in that sort of thing. The day is so hot you must feel like coolin' down a little."

The beach. The idea sounded good. The day was really hot and she knew the beach could do a better job at cooling her down than the shower. But thinking back on yesterday, she was sure it would be a bad idea. Albert wouldn't like to know she was out on the beach with some man — even if this man was his friend.

The place was terribly hot though.

"I'm not interested," she said. "I have some things to start doin' before Albert come home..."

"Like what?"

"Well, like him dinner," she said.

"Oh, come on! We won't be that long. We'll just be there till the sun go away a little. You'll be back with more than enough time for dinner. I'll even buy you lunch — fish an' festivals — you'll love it!"

She had a good feeling she would. That was what she was afraid of, too. John seemed like a very nice guy to be around. He was often times very funny as she came to realise whenever he came by to see Albert. They would sit outside while she remained in her room for Albert didn't want her to be too much into his friends lest they started to think that she was leading them on. Albert would just be laughing uncontrollably for the most part as John talked on and on about some wild story. It could be about anything really, it was just his way of talking about it that made it sound like he was successfully trying to give jokes. "You mus' be jokin'," Albert would say from time to time and John would say, "Serious as a judge." Christine could always hear his wife laughing at his jokes. Dionne always seemed happy with him, Christine just knew that he ate pussy as well — only men who did that got women to smile so often.

She now wondered if this was another one of Albert's tests. Was he trying to see what she would do if a man came to ask her out? Probably he was on the beach waiting to see what the result was going to be. Christine wasn't willing to take that chance. Or was she? She had been planning to leave not long ago and only the letter to Princess changed her mind...so what now? Should she probably let him think this was indeed the way to start being defiant? She really didn't want to hurt him anymore than the other woman had. Christine cared enough to know that hurting him even a little bit might give him enough reason to not want to go on anymore. It was the sad truth.

As if reading her mind, John said, "Albert didn't put me up to this if that's what you're thinking. I just thought you might do well goin' out a little instead of being holed up here like this. Ever been to Hellshire?"

"No," she said.

"Well this is you big chance. An' don't be afraid of me for I'm not goin' to do anything foolish. I'm what you call a nice guy, the ones that finish last in high school an' have to do all the dirty work because they are supposed to help people out."

"You think I'm dirty work?"

"Far from," he said, "far, far from."

Christine smiled. Even when she listened to him talking to Albert from her room, he had this effect on her. It was like a sort of magic. She looked away and across at the parking lot. The heat flowed like the ocean, just inches above the asphalt. "Will we get back before four?"

"Sure!" John said. He was now fairly convinced she was beginning to see the outing a real possibility. "I promise we'll be back by three-fifteen, the latest. We'll just get a dip in the water, have lunch and head back. By then, the sun should be all the way over there." He pointed east first then west. Christine smiled again.

"An' that's all we goin' to do?" She wanted to be sure.

"I have too much to lose," he said.

"Give me five minutes," she told him.

"Sure."

Twenty-One

His car was what they saw first as they returned from the beach. It was parked in its usual place only not at the usual time. Albert was almost two and a half hours early. Just like he was yesterday, she thought. Christine didn't know what to make of this fact. Was he going to try the same shit he did yesterday? No, she wasn't going to allow it. She wasn't expecting such a change of his plans on a random day such as this. But then, with Albert, one should really expect anything at any time. That was what he wanted her to think too. That way she wouldn't do anything stupid. She wasn't thinking that what she had done was stupid. She had gone to the beach with a friend to cool off a little. Nothing more. If he wanted to let that be a problem to him, too bad. He didn't like her cussing at the top of her voice, but today she thought she would do just that if he went too far. He would also probably get angry and cuss all he wanted to, but he would get over it for she knew…he loved her. Yes, she knew this — he didn't have any other reason to treat her the way he did — but he was very afraid of what it might do to him.

"Oh shit," John said and exasperated. He turned off the engine and slumped back in his seat.

"Don't worry 'bout it," Christine told him, as cool and calm as the time at the beach had made her. "It nuh as bad as it look."

John looked across at her. She was still in the two-piece bathsuit — she never took any other form of clothing with her. The towel made a skirt round her. There was sand on her feet and along her hairline and behind her ears and under her neck.

"You sound so sure," John said.

"Mi sure," she said, "We talk the other day an' him say it alright fi go out sometime." She didn't believe a word she was saying but she tried to sound convincing. The last thing she would want right now was for John to start regretting that he had taken her out. She had enjoyed herself more than she had in a long time and she was not prepared for anyone to feel sorry for that happening. She got out of the car. John followed. He locked up and they both walked down the pathway till they got to his place where he turned off while she continued to the next gate.

When Christine opened the door Albert was seated in the sofa with his face in his hands. He was crying. Christine walked past him to her room. He was really a fucking weirdo, she thought. She went out with someone and here he is bawling away like a little pussy. She washed herself in the shower and put on a housedress before coming back out. This time, he was seated in the sofa, staring at the door as though he wasn't even seeing it, looking miles away.

Where were you? She thought of him saying. How much time I must tell you not to leave without me? Eh, Christine?

"She gone," was all Albert said without looking at her.

Christine knew in an instant he wasn't talking about her. It was his mother. She sat down beside him.

"I'm sorry," she said. He had told her just days ago that his mother was getting worse and that he felt he needed to stay longer at the hospital with her. He had made her some soup all by himself this morning. He wanted to do it for he wanted to be able to do something for her in her last days. Anything he could, "Did you get to talk to her before..."

Albert shook his head and wiped his eyes. He heard people speak of it all the time but it never really happened to him till today. He knew his mother wouldn't make it but he never thought it would have been so soon. He was always hoping she would be blessed with a few more months at least. But as time passed and he kept going to the hospital to see her, he was almost sure she wasn't going to make it that long. But somewhere inside him, Albert still hoped she would. It seemed things got a lot worse very fast for yesterday when he went to see her what he saw frightened him. She had lost so much weight she wasn't even able to sit up by herself. The pastor from her church came to see her along with another long time church friend and they prayed for her. While they were there, Albert could see it in their eyes — just as they could see it in his — that she wasn't going to be with them much longer. Then he looked around him in the ward and realised that no one there seemed to be looking as though they were going to get out. This he thought, was the End of the Road Ward — only the doctors never got around to telling you straight out. They skirted the issue for as long as they could maybe because they themselves couldn't stand the damned bawling ("In two weeks I'll be transferred out of here. Let the other intern deliver the bad news"). Yesterday, he asked one doctor about her condition and he did say she was very weak and wouldn't be around much longer but Albert was thinking a few days at least. Not one night. When he got there this morning and saw the empty bed he began shaking uncontrollably for he knew too well what that meant. Unrealistically, he was hoping that she was somewhere around, maybe gone for an X-Ray or something like that. But he knew very well that Ester's days of X-raying were long behind her. There was nothing left to see.

"Would you like a seat, sir?" A sturdy nurse had asked him and had to help him to the chair almost instantly for he was falling when she started asking the question.

"Where is she?" he had asked. He took the glass of water she offered.

"I am sorry, sir," she told him for she knew he knew.

"Oh God, no." The thermos with the soup almost fell from his hands and the nurse took it from him and rested it on her desk.

After leaving the hospital, Albert went to the church his mother used to attend. They were having a midday service for her. When he got in, the pastor was asking God to take her into his mighty arms and rebuke the illness. It was too late for that. They didn't wait for him to tell them to start crying. The moment they saw Albert enter the door they knew. The crying then became much louder than the prayers they had been sending to God. He didn't bother to go to work any money after that. He simply stayed at the church for a while and then came right home.

"I didn't do enough," he said.

"Yuh do everythin' yuh coulda do," Christine said. She held his hand. He didn't object. He didn't seem to know. Christine kissed his cheek. Albert didn't object to this, either. It was as if he was begging her to comfort him only he would never come out and say it. But she knew he wanted it so she kissed his lips next and he held onto her for dear life as her tongue found his.

They remained like this for about a minute, eating at each other's mouth and face and neck. It was something they both wanted but never brought themselves to do. Christine thought about George momentarily but then the kisses stole her thoughts. Albert groaned and leaned over her. She could feel his bulging cock. George shot in her mind again and what stuck was what he would be doing next if he were the one here now kissing her. So much did this thought captivate her mind that she held onto Albert's head and coaxed it down to her crotch. As she did this, she waited for him to pull away and tell her how rude she was but he didn't. Instead, she felt his tongue rooting beneath her panties and licking at the now wet slit between her legs. Christine caressed his hair and leaned back as she enjoyed the sensation he gave her.

It wasn't long after this that she came, her eyes fluttering open just in time to see Albert pulling his hard cock from his pants. She quickly let go of him and pulled herself to the other end of the sofa. Albert came at her like a wild beast but she successfully held him off. "We shouldn't do this," she said, panting.

"Why not?" Albert asked. He sounded as desperate as a man begging for his life, his force never relenting. "Is that damn George, don't?" He asked.

Albert let go of her and got up. He paced the room slowly. Should he tell her what he saw this morning? Or rather, who he saw this morning? Just tell her and let her see that this man she held so dearly was actually living somewhere with somebody else and possibly the biological father of that little boy that ran to greet him?

"Mi don't know what this George have make you worship him so much," Albert said finally and went into the bathroom. After about five minutes, he came out and left the house. She could hear his car come alive and pull out.

Twenty-Two

"Christine!"

Christine awoke because Albert was knocking on the door and calling her name. She rose and glanced at the clock on the wall. It glowed, 3:15 AM.

"Yes?" She said, irritated.

"Christine, are you awake?"

"Now. What is it?" She asked.

"There's... I'm comin' in."

Before she could respond, the door came slowly open and Albert stepped in and came to her bedside where he sat. Christine sat up as she didn't like the feel of him hanging over her like that.

"There's something I've been meanin' to ask you but it slipped me earlier because of everything that happen'. Why did you go to the beach with John? Why yuh didn't ask me to take you?"

"Me did hot an' him say him woulda carry mi so mi go. You was not here an' mi never think nothing wrong with that."

"But couldn't you think that him might want you and I wouldn't want him to have you? Suppose he got the better of you when you were in his car, what would happen to us now?"

"Stop thinking like that," she said. "You should not be thinking about him, think about me. What do I want? What do I feel? If I don't want him to do that to me him can't unless him rape mi so stop thinking like that. The bottom line is if I want him too you can't do nutten unless you plan to kill one a' we. So stop worryin' yuh head over nothin'."

"Don't go there. I wouldn't even think of doin' that. Before I do that, I think I'd prefer —"

"Kill yourself?"

His eyes came wide open and his face went pale.

"Mi see the letter in the diary," she said. "I read every word of it an' I think you did the right thing by not carryin' it out. No one is worth that, Albert. Not me, not her. No one."

"Yeah, I guess you right."

"Mi right yes, an' yuh know it," she insisted.

"So what do I do now?" He asked. Outside a dog started barking in the distance. Another caught on soon enough and closer still others joined in. Now it was like the dogs next door were barking too, sending whatever communication it was to all the others in Portmore.

"You stop worryin' so much and live free," she told him.

"Can..." Albert paused and thought for a short while. "Can you help me?"

This was when Christine reached over and hugged him close. "Mi t'ink yuh woulda neva ask," she said.

Twenty-Three

Albert's mother's funeral was the following weekend. Christine and a few neighbours accompanied him. John couldn't make it for he'd left for work on the ship the Wednesday before but Dionne was there. It was a sombre occasion with much sobbing for the dearly departed lady. "She was a pillar of strength in her community," the presiding minister said. "She brought into this world children who grew up to become responsible citizens, always knowing a sense of right and wrong, and seeming to always choose the former."

After the proceedings, they went back home and Christine made dinner. They ate slowly as Albert thought about all that had happened.

With a few hours left before the end of the evening, they went out to see a movie. It had been years since Albert set foot into a cinema but, with Christine's advice, he decided that he would go see one today. Live a little. It proved to be quite entertaining and he wondered at the end of it all why he had never gone out to see some sooner.

He was now allowing Christine to call anybody she wanted to from his phone and have anybody she wanted call her. Still, the only calls she made were to her home in Macca Tree to talk to Jodi and Matilda. On one of these, she was told something that made her heart skip a beat or two. George had called and said he was coming home soon.

"Soon, Granny?" she asked. "Him nuh say how soon?"

"Soon," Matilda's voice said with some arrogance. "Him seh soon an' da's all yuh need fi know."

Christine thought she wouldn't say anything to Albert. By now, he was already comfortable with the idea that she had a man and that he was going to come home to her some day soon. Well, he seemed comfortable but she knew better. It was killing him inside for he truly wanted her for himself. Christine knew this. She didn't want him to get hurt and she wished she could tell him not to worry for he won't but she couldn't and she knew it.

She was having mixed feelings about George. If he still wanted her, she thought she would want him too. He called from Canada just as often as he used to when he just got there. George didn't like to spend money so when he went out of his way to make one hour calls from that far away, he really had an interest in whomever he was calling.

She was also quite certain she cared for Albert. He took care of her and she was getting to understand who he was and why he was that way. She wondered, if she had to leave, would he stay strong and go on with life as if she never misled him? Or would he think she was just like Princess who set him up to let him down? Christine didn't have the answers. But in time, she was sure, they would all be revealed.

Twenty-Four

Two days later, she had an unexpected visitor. Christine didn't see him come in. This was because he watched from the roof till she was around the front sweeping the small yard space before crawling down and entering through the door on the far side. He waited patiently in the kitchen while she finished up what she was doing. While there, he got undressed and treated himself to some soda from the fridge. It was a Pepsi. He didn't like Pepsi but that was all that was there. *Just my luck*, he thought. He found some corn bread and had that too.

Christine came in humming the tune of a song he didn't know. She opened the fridge and quickly realised something was terribly wrong. She froze, looking at everything in it like seeing them for the first time.

"Ah dis yuh a look fa?" The male voice asked from somewhere behind her. Snatch came up quickly and covered her mouth with a coarse hand. Christine started kicking and trying to break free but then he held her tighter and forced her to the living room where he pushed her to the sofa and laid on her. The next thing she saw was the big gun he was rudely introducing to her face. "If yuh scream a bus' yuh raas skull," he said. "Yuh hear me?"

Christine nodded several times. The man who raped her over seven years ago was at his tricks again and she was seemingly without an option.

"Mi know say yuh memba mi," Snatch said, his breath rancid in her nostrils. "Gall Bladda! Dem call mi Snatch now but mi a di same man. Same way mi get yuh uppa Macca Tree, same way mi can get yuh dung yah soh, jus' like dat. Yuh might even did a t'ink yuh want fi kill mi from long time an' now mi have yuh like dis again when yuh a big woman now. Yuh nah wonda why God so fuckin' wicked to yuh? Why him mek a' ol' fart like me can get yuh when him want so much time? Yuh nuh ask yuhself dat?"

Christine nodded for, though her lips were now free, she could not speak.

"Open yuh legs," Snatch commanded.

Reluctantly, Christine did as he said. She really couldn't believe this was happening to her again and by the same man. That's why the tears started streaming down her cheeks. She really wanted to kill him. Kill him and end this nightmare once and for all.

Snatch looked and smiled. He ran the barrel of the gun over it, sticking it lightly to see the mound pit like pressing on an inflated balloon. "Still look good." He pulled away the panties and took a peek. The metal felt sickly cool as it touched her bare skin. Snatch nodded. "Still look good."

He then got up from off her and walked to the window. He looked out and then back at Christine. "Anyway, a nuh dat mi come fa so yuh can relax." he said and sat in the love seat. "A talk mi waan talk to yuh. Mi nuh waan yuh fi say nutten. Jus' listen, alright?"

Christine nodded, not once taking her eyes off him.

"The guys round here think me is some kind ah hero," Snatch began, "action man who always know the right thing to do an' say. Dem t'ink I kill people too nuff to mention an' I really don't mind dem thinkin' this 'cause it make me feel like is true. Fact of the matter is I is a rapist an' a thief. Dere is nothin' else I ever do that wrong but that. I is not the don in prison either. Not like I let them believe, at least." He continued:

"The last time mi go prison, the man dem hold me dung an give mi some bloodclaat fuck! Mi seh mi would a never want to go back deh fi nutten at all. The administration change up in there now. All sorts of things happen. Me don't intend to go back in there. An' mi mean it. Especially now that I start feelin' sick an' go doctor last week. The news bad. At least for me it not good, but for you it might be the best news you hearin' in eight years. That's why me think me would come by an' let you know."

Snatch paused and started pulling his clothes back on. "So you can see that I could let you get what I have but I goin' to spare you an' let you live to feel good about what happen to me. Nuh dat yuh want?"

Christine didn't respond.

"Feel good because you want to kill mi from God know when? Mi can only think that mi deserve it after what me do to you an' a few others like you. Me shouldn' go back ah jail that last time for it prove one time too much...the man dem seh mi go a road an' go get sexy pon dem so them have to deal with me case." He chuckled. "Yuh believe that? Me couldn' even walk good for two or so days after dem done. An' now me health is goin' downhill fast. Mi don't have to tell you what wrong with me. You mus' know." He put the gun in his waistband and turned to leave her. "Mi jus' think you should know that."

Christine watched him walk away. Then he stopped and without turning asked, "So was it a boy or a girl? You can answer this one."

"Girl," Christine said.

"She must be quite pretty," he said. "You is a pretty woman... sexy an' pretty."

"...She is."

"Say hi to her for me." Then he left.

After he was gone, Christine broke down and cried.

Twenty-Five

Christine went home to Macca Tree that weekend and learned that George had come home. Albert was not able to take her for he had work to do but he never had a problem with her coming up all alone these days. He was trying very hard to make her feel less caged in. He wanted to try to be the man she wanted him to be — the man that, possibly, Princess wanted him to be too. Only then, he was too set in the belief that he was who he was and couldn't change. He knew better now. You could always change and bad habits, especially, were worth revising every now and then.

Matilda told her that George was waiting for her down by his parents' house. Christine felt both happy and confused at the same time. It would be good to see him again after so long, but she also wondered, why now? Him here now only made everything more complicated. She thought she needed some time to sort herself out, be certain just who it was that she wanted to be with. Now, she really wasn't certain.

She did go to see him though and the moment she saw his face she started feeling all that emotion welling inside her again, just like when he was here the last time. This was just not going to be easy for her and she knew it.

"Hi, baby," he said.

"Hi," she said.

"You look good."

"...Thanks," she said.

George tried to kiss her but she pulled away. Albert was on her mind and it bothered her. He was giving in so much to her now that she didn't want to hurt him like this. It felt like she was...cheating on him.

"No," she said and let go of his hand.

"What?" He couldn't believe what was happening.

"I can't do this."

"Wh-what you mean you can't do this? Are you tellin' me you don't want this anymore? Is that what you tellin' me, Christine? After all we been through?"

"That's not what I'm sayin'," she said.

"What are you sayin' then?"

"I'm sayin' I can't do this. That's all. Not right now."

George furrowed his brows and thought for a while. "It's that man you workin' for isn't it? He's finally gotten to you like I predicted. Right?"

Christine didn't answer.

"I'll beat the shit out of him," he said.

"What?" Christine asked.

"If him love you that much then he'll be willin' to fight for you. I'll fight for you right now because I love you. If he feels the same way, he will fight me. Whoever win get the girl. Just like in the movies. Simple as that. What yuh think?"

"No," she said. She would never really want that to happen at all. The thrill of two men fighting to win her love was quite romantic but not very practical. It reminded her of those early days when George beat that boy Richard Timble. What was a man if he couldn't fight for the woman he loved? Nothing but a man frame, she thought. Still she didn't think Albert was quite the match up for a man the size of George.

"If you nuh want the fight, leave him now an' come back to me. Yuh willin' to do that?"

She was silent.

"Alright the fight is on, you can tell him when you see him. Tell him seh Macca George ah go mash up him rass. Yuh hear me?"

"But if you even fight him an' beat him up, mi not comin' back to you," she said.

"Yuh will come back. If me beat him up fi you an' yuh nuh come back to me, then you is a fuckin' fool."

Twenty-Six

"Dead?" She asked Albert, truly frightened.

"Dead," Albert told her.

"How?" She asked, not wanting to sound too anxious. She never mentioned to Albert that Snatch was the father of her child and she hoped Snatch never got around to saying it to anyone either. As far as she knew, Albert only knew that she was aware that Snatch was an ex-convict and someone who should not be trusted at all. That was all.

"Sort of strange how they seh it happen. Him apparently t'ief money from the Texaco gas station and police chase him and corner him just out by Phase Two entrance there. Mi hear say them ask him to drop him gun an' give up. He didn't. Instead, him run toward dem, shoutin', 'Kill mi, kill mi,' till shots from the police them put him down like a wild animal." Albert paused, shaking his head. "It was just so strange, as if he wanted to die, I hear. A man like Snatch, I would think him would want to live to do more wrongs but I guess not. Is like the devil was callin' him home after a long life of service. I've heard that that man has raped a number of women and robbed houses. I guess yuh could seh him deserve what him get."

"Oh God!" Christine went and shook her head. She seemed very contemplative.

"You're actin' like yuh sorry for him Do you know how many lives him destroy with his terrible ways? You should understand more than anybody else, you were raped at some point in your life, too and you never liked it, did you? If he was the one that do it to you, I bet you wouldn't be actin' this way now. You'd probably want to kill him yourself."

"Probably," she said. But nothing could get the thought from her mind that the father of her child was gunned down by the police. She knew he was bad, but did he deserve it? To go out like that?

Yet, in another part of her mind — the part that closed doors and opened others Christine felt relieved. It was like the world had opened up once again and she could go and do any thing she wanted to without feeling the fear of someone hurting her. Gall Bladda was out of the world and it made her feel much better inside.

"Albert," she said, "mi have sup'm to tell you."

Twenty-Seven

"Do what?" Albert asked. He looked at her for a long time after this, not quite sure what else to say. Christine told him everything, from who Snatch really was to her to the fact that George was back in town. All Albert could think of now though was that George was planning to beat the shit out of him, "Fight me?"

"That's what him say," she said. "Mi try to talk him out of it but him sound serious..."

"So why him woulda want to do a thing like that?"

She said, "Him seh me an' you deh."

"Is that you tell him? Say me and you deh?"

"No, is him just think so because me never want him kiss me," she said and added, "Me nuh think me love him again. Ah yuh mi love now."

Albert came over and kissed her. She did not resist.

"What a time to declare you feelin'," he said. "So you tell him you don't love him too?"

Christine shook her head.

"Why not?"

"Mi never sure before mi see him again but mi sure now."

He kissed her again.

Is what this me get miself into now God? Albert asked himself. At this point, he thought about telling her about where he saw George but he didn't. It wasn't that important right now. Maybe some other time, he thought.

"Mi try to tell him that not necessary," she repeated, "but him insist."

Albert paced the room as he thought some more. George wanted to fight him. The man he saw was quite huge. In fact, he seemed pretty fit and strong. He remembered the way he picked up the woman like she was a fifty-pound sack of rice and threw her over his shoulder — and when he did that he also had a child standing on his shoe! But was he just going to let the size of this man scare 'im off from having the woman he wanted? Maybe for another woman...but this woman saved his life! He felt that the least he could do was win her fair and square.

"You set him up to this, Christine?" Albert asked, feeling very uneasy about the whole thing at this point. "Why didn't you tell me he is in the country before you went off to see him? Makin' big plans for me, were you?"

"No! I wasn't makin' any plans. I wouldn't do that! Him come without me knowin' either. I was shocked when dem tell mi him here. You can just tell him you aren't interested in that. I'll love you still."

"Why? Don't you think I'm man enough to handle myself in a fight? If that's the case, you probably don't think I'm man enough to do anything else either. He will always have that over my head like my lowest moment. It better I go and fight and lose, than not fight and have him swing that over me for eternity."

"But him big you know an' him do some boxin' from time to time."

"Boxin'?"

"Yes, him go gym an dem things deh. Him will knock you out if yuh not careful."

"I don't want to hear any of that. No matter how big him is or bad, him is a man just like me and that mean him can get beat up too. I just have to be smart enough and know what I'm doin' when him come at me that's all."

"Alright then, if you say so," she said.

"Tell me though," Albert said, "if mi fight him an' lose, you goin' to want me still?"

"Yes."

"Yuh sure?" He asked.

"Sure," she said.

"Well, that's it then," Albert said. "Anytime him ready."

*****

The worry came later that night while he was alone in bed. He hadn't been in a fight since high school and almost lost that one if his then girlfriend hadn't intercepted a fist from the guy named Spuddy Ranks who would have crippled him with that left hook. Now he was to be up against another supposedly biggy and he was just wondering what he was getting himself into. A big mistake, that's what it was.

"A big mistake," Albert said under his breath. He wasn't even sure when George was going to come get him. He guessed he just had to start getting prepared for him any day now. He was going to start training and get everything back in full working order. He was tired of being the Coward of the County. He was going to be the hero — the James Bond who always walked away with the girl at the end of the movie. Come what may.

Twenty-Eight

Macca George punched the bag of sand he had hanging from a mango tree in his backyard. He had put it up the very day Christine told him of her desires to be with that damned Albert. It had been a while since he'd done any real fighting. That was going to change.

He was sweating for he'd been slugging at the bag for over thirty minutes now. Before this, he had done some skipping and jogging. When preparing for an official fight, he would normally do his routine in three-minute sets. But this fight would have no rounds. It was going to be one big brawl. He, however, intended to pulverize Albert within the first three minutes anyway.

So what if he had another woman and kids? Christine was his. He waited so long, so patiently to have her and under no circumstance was he going to just let her slip away from him like that — not to some new kid on the block who apparently had a bag of tricks up his sleeves. Not a rass!

Christine liked the way he beat the shit out of Timble back in school. He was going to do the same to Albert and hoped she viewed it in the same light. Show her that he still had it in him.

Each time George hit the bag, he thought of it as Albert's gut. He liked punching guys in the stomach and watching them fold over his big fist.

He was going to go pay Albert a visit in the morning. The sooner the better, he thought.

Alex Morgan

Getting the address had been easy. He simply had the taxi driver that took Christine to Spanish Town follow her to Portmore just to see the house she was staying at. That same taxi driver would take him there. He'd thought of asking Matilda for the address but she probably wouldn't have given it to him. And even if she did, she would quite likely tell Christine and that might mean Albert realising just how imminent his arsing was going to be. George didn't want that. The element of surprise was crucial in these encounters. Just like he had surprised Timble. He didn't do too well in the scheduled fights where everybody knew where and when it was going to happen. He didn't know whether Albert could fight or what he looked like but it was safe to assume he could. Assume he could fight just like those guys who kept knocking him out when he was on the verge of making the big times. Those guys who took his dream away from him. Those Mean Steve Greens. To George, Albert represented all of those guys and he was going to make him pay for what they did.

Macca George finished training at six thirty that evening. He then got a shower and went to bed early so he could be super fresh for his encounter in the morning.

*****

While George slept and dreamt about victory, Albert was up in his room shadow boxing. He had gone to the bookstore and bought a book called *Boxing Made Simple*. He read its fifty pages in less than an hour and soon started practicing what it said. Bobbing and weaving as the instructions suggested, Albert worked up a sweat. It was funny, but the longer he worked at it the less tired he felt. In fact, what he felt right now was horny. Christine was asleep in her room. He thought of going over and begging her for some action but then thought not. There was a time for every thing and right now he strongly believed he needed to get himself prepared for this fight. For after all, George might just decide to come get him in the morning. Who knows?

"Bob an' weave," he told himself as he skipped and danced like a boxer in his little space. "Bob an' weave."

It was sheer exhaustion that knocked him out at about 1:30 a.m.

Twenty-Nine

6:17 AM

Albert woke up with a jolt. No sooner than he did he went to his window and looked out. All was well. No stranger lurking out by his gate, ready to bum rush him.

He stretched, went back to bed and dreamed about fucking Christine.

If he knew that while he looked out the window Macca George was just leaving his house to catch the cab he chartered to take him to Braeton, Albert probably would have started practicing again.

Thirty

8:25 AM

"Ah who di rass name Albert?"

The sound came with a boom into the house. Christine who was laying in the sofa, reading a math text, sat bolt upright. "George!" She said under her breath.

"Jesus Christ!" Albert went. He was at the microwave; just about taking out a piece of pizza he warmed for a quick snack before breakfast. The pizza fell from his hand and splattered on the floor, looking like vomit in one hard chunk. Pieces of mushroom and pepperoni danced all about the crust like spilt coins. He was just sizing up Christine and wondering what she would do if he tried to carry out his dream now. He guessed he'd have to find that out another time.

Albert paced frantically, trying to remember just what he'd told himself he would do if and when this arose. *Bob an' weave, Albert*, he told himself, *bob an' weave*. The fight exercises would be handy at this time, he knew, but could he remember them? Was she really worth it? These questions confronted him like darts sailing at a bullseye. Was she really worth it? Really now?

She was.

"Albert?" The man's voice boomed again. It was now followed by a thump on the front door. He was now at the front door — Albert's front door! Jesus Christ! He must have jumped the gate.

Albert was sure he locked it last night before coming in. Either that or George just stepped over it like it wasn't there. He did seem tall enough. Or maybe he ripped it off it's hinges, Albert, a voice told him. George looks like the man to do a thing like that. Can you imagine what he can do to you?

Albert didn't know this, but people were looking out. Not coming out, for they didn't want to get caught in the middle of some terrible thing. Many of them were still shaken by the shooting incident that left Snatch dead — not that they didn't think he deserved it. So now they didn't want to just go out like that and maybe get into trouble. Curtains parted from cracked windows but you couldn't see their eyes. Those were still in the dark of their little houses. Those little houses that held so many secrets of their own. Those little houses that you couldn't get out of if the grills were locked and you couldn't find the keys. Those little houses that you just couldn't get out of that easily. No backdoors to escape through. *Jesus Christ.. .No escape!*

Albert tried to stay calm. "What mi goin' to do now?" He asked loud enough for Christine to hear. He didn't even remember she was there with him. He felt alone. Very alone.

"Christine, you in deh wid di coward? Him nuh waa fight fi yuh da's why him a bloodclaat hide!" The voice continued.

"Is...is who that?" Albert went. He tried to sound strong but it wasn't working and he knew it.

"Yuh nuh know a who? Yuh betta open dis door before mi kick it off." With this came a loud thud against the door. It rattled on its hinges. Another one like that and it might just come falling in.

Albert farted. The heat was getting to him somewhat and he was beginning to feel faint. Either that or he was really feeling like a coward. Was she really worth it? He asked himself again. Was she?

She was, he yet again concluded. She was worth it.

"George, just go home nuh," Christine said. "Why you mus' think yuh have to do all this?"

"Mi not goin' up till you come wid me. If him win di fight, him can keep you. Come out an' fight yuh rass bait! Stop hide behind di gal frack tail an' come stan' up like a fuckin' man."

Some persons were coming out now. One thing they realized was that the violence seemed to be directed only at Albert. Further, there didn't seem to be a gun in the play so they could scurry back to their box homes if necessary with time to spare.

"Mi a goh out deh," Albert said to himself and started for the door.

Christine held onto his hand. "No! Him will kill yuh," she told him. But Albert pulled free and walked on anyway.

As he walked, he took some time to get to the door. That was because his mind was racing so fast it was going past real time. He was thinking of what he was about to get himself into. *Bob an' weave, bob an' weave.* He also thought that this was happening to him all over again. A love triangle. He was an ass.

"Come out man!" George shouted.

"Wait!" Albert shouted at the door. *Bob an' weave, bob an' weave.* He was sounding strong and bold now. He didn't feel that way though but he was trying to convince himself to. "Kill yuh claat out deh today."

There was no sound on the other side now. It was as though the other man was reflecting on what was said. Albert was sounding like a real bully. That wasn't going to stop anything though for George had his mind made up already.

Albert's mind was made up too. He wasn't going to back down now. He was going to fight for the woman that had given him a reason to not kill himself. *Bob an' weave, bob an' weave.* If he died in the process that would be quite ironic — but at least it wouldn't be suicide.

Or would it?

Albert turned the lock and went outside. The man was taller than him by about four inches. He was also huge. Very huge. It seemed to be cut out for a David and Goliath show-down. This was no Bible story though. Goliath might just win this time, Albert thought. The rematch was two thousand years in the making and now he could hear a commentator saying, *let's get ready to rumbleeee!* It's the fight dubbed the Barbarian in Braeton.

George smiled when he saw the man finally appear. Other persons gathered to see just what this fateful day would bring. It seemed somebody would be pulverized. Some residents saw when Albert stepped out and thought of saying something but then thought no. The last thing they would want was for the big giant to turn on them too. If things got really bad — really, really bad — they probably would try something for Albert was a member of the community, but they all thought they would hang back and remain safe for a while. Besides, Albert should know what he was getting into when he decided to walk out that door.

Albert was sweating profusely. His forehead was glossy. He wasn't going to say another word to the man across the way and he knew the man would quite likely be thinking the same thing. It was now time for action. He made a few steps closer to his fate and stopped.

This was when George started for him. He stepped hurriedly as if he didn't want to waste much time doing this. Get it over with as quickly as possible and return to life as normal with his girl, Christine.

Christine was coming at him, George saw. She ran past Albert who was swaying somewhat and charged at George, apparently attempting to push him away from the fight. "No, George," she was shouting. "Don't bother with this."

"Move out a mi way!" George went and pushed her aside. She fell sprawling. Some young boys who were standing nearby instinctively angled their heads to see if they could get a glimpse of her underwear or just how much buffer she had between her legs. The way she fell, though, didn't give much away. But when she tried to get up and fell again, this time on her back, they saw it all. Some turned away grinning. Their eyes bright and their young cocks hard for they had seen the beauty of the world all in one fleeting glance. They saw black underwear covering a pussy that seemed to fill the fabric to its capacity. "Fat, eeeh?" One of them said. The others nodded, wide-eyed.

George grabbed onto Albert and hooked an upper cut under his right rib cage. Albert's knees buckled but he wasn't allowed to fall for George held him well. He cracked him one again. This time it was squarely in the gut. Albert felt like shitting himself but that didn't happen, thank God. At least, he didn't think so. It was hard to tell when so much else was happening to his body in these initial seconds of what was scheduled for twelve rounds.

"Give him a chance!" a lady was shouting from somewhere close by. Albert heard this but he also heard everything else. They were all begging the big man not to kill him. This gave Albert, if he needed it, a fair idea of just who was winning this round. At one point, he found himself free of George's grip and what he did shocked even him. He ran toward the giant and hugged onto him for dear life. He was forgetting that he could run away. Run away because it could very well save his life to the looks of things. But what Albert was really thinking, strangely enough, was that he was in a ring and the people paid good money to see this thing through and by God he was going to stay in that ring. Round one was bad but he could get over it in round two — if it ever came. It should be coming any moment now. The first round was beginning to seem like an eternity to him.

Then reality hit home. It came in the form of a kick to his groin. As he felt his bladder tighten with the pain, he remembered this was not an organised fight. It was a street brawl and anything went. Anything!

This was when he bit hard into George's crotch. He felt the bulge in his mouth and thinking that for months — probably years — after this, they would be teasing him with names like *Man Eater*. That didn't stop him though for he was making George cry out.

Albert bit harder still till George's hands were strapped onto his head, trying to pull it from the enflamed area. Albert bit harder. The big man fell to his knees, crying. It seemed all his energy was gone and he just couldn't hit Albert anymore. Even his grip on Albert's head felt lame. The cheers now were, "Yeahhhhh! Albert show di big bwoy seh yuh wicked a' dan him!" However, there were others who said, "Da bredda deh col' eh? 'Im bite di yute pon 'im buddy!"

When Albert did release George, the big man wasn't even able to get up. He looked drained. Albert kicked him in the gut repeatedly. He felt like he could really pull this off now. He couldn't stop kicking the man. There was suddenly more energy in him and he was going to use it to kill George. Kill him out of principle. Kill him because nerdy birdie Jason and Princess nearly killed him. The feeling was quite liberating too.

People did come eventually to pull him off George before he got into real trouble. But this didn't happen till they were quite satisfied that George got all he deserved. In their minds, it seemed, he deserved a whole lot.

As Albert walked away, he held Christine by one hand and literally pulled her along. The crowd that gathered was now shouting, "Albert! Albert! Albert!" He carried Christine inside and kicked the door shut on the cheering masses. He never spoke.

"Albert what's wrong?" Christine asked, but he said nothing still. Albert stopped walking when he got to his bedroom and with an unexpected turn, pushed Christine to his bed. She bounced momentarily. He stood there looking at her for a while as she steadied herself and gazed up at the man who said nothing at all since beating George.

She knew though. She knew what was going to happen now. Albert was ready. His eyes were telling her that he was going to fuck her silly and she deserved it. All of it. She felt a little scared considering this would be her very first in a long time, but she wasn't going to back down. Not now. She was willing to take all he had to give.

Albert loosened his big brown belt and pulled his zipper and button. She could hear the sound of the zipper even above the commotion outside. It sounded like a musical note and the jingle of the belt buckle added to the tune of sex. She watched as he unleashed his cock to the open air. It sprang forth from the confines of his boxers like a mad boa constrictor. The head got bigger and darker as it throbbed to full attention. It was salivating. So was she.

Albert came toward her and she slid down the bed to meet him. This action caused her skirt to ride up all the way to the swell of her hips. He was now seeing what the youngsters saw when George flashed her away. She could see his cock throb with much more energy and its red head was now a dark maroon. Christine came forward and took it in her mouth. Gently at first as she got used to the salty taste and musky odour. It was the cock of a winner. A champion.

The man trembled and pulled away sharply as if struck by volts of electricity. She held onto it and then looked up at him. Slowly, she guided it back to her warm mouth and took it in a little at a time. She wasn't sure what experienced girls did with it but she took it in anyway. Her mouth watered for the delicacy. Her pussy ached for every inch of it. She hoped she could manage.

Albert backed away again. "No, no," he whispered. "Can't stand anymore."

Christine eased back and he leaned over her, balancing on one hand as the other pulled away the fabric that was now soaking wet. He didn't need to hold his cock for it was hard enough to jack hammer a paved road. It found the tight entrance with much ease. The pressure was applied steadily. Christine clenched her teeth and held her breath for she knew it was coming any time now. Pain more than she would want but she wasn't going to stop for she also wanted the sweetness of his cock. She tried to relax but couldn't.

Albert muscled his way into her pussy. It was hot and tight still. He tried to be gentle but was so damned horny he just knew he was doing it a little too hard sometimes. She would cringe as he tried to sink himself deeper inside her. 'When she did this, he kissed her tenderly and slowed down.

With each thrust, Christine felt like she was falling without a parachute. This was one reason she held him round his back. It was a feeling like she had never experienced before. George should have been the one two years ago but he missed and she was glad. She just hoped Albert liked doing this sort of thing for she would need it a lot from now on. She just knew she'd be shouting things like, "Fuck me! Fuck out me pussy!" and he'd be asking, "Ah whose?" and she'd say, "Ah fi yuh! Fuck it! Fuck out it rass!" Albert Bench loved all this for she had changed him. For now, though, she just moaned and shut her eyes tight.

"Albert! Albert! Albert!" He could hear the crowd cheering. Either they were still doing it or it was stuck in his mind. He couldn't tell for sure but either way it spurred him on. He could feel his scrotum tightening, as he got ready to explode inside her. Albert was now grunting like a wild boar. He tried to control himself a little for he knew Christine was still feeling some pain, but everytime he slowed down she pulled him in. She wanted him to fuck her. Fuck her hard. And that was good for now as his cock was becoming a volcano and he couldn't help himself. Albert rammed his cock all the way up in Christine's pussy time and again in quick succession till he exploded. "Agh! Agh! Agh!!" He went as he collapsed on top of her. She wrapped her legs around him and squeezed.

"Albert! Albert! Albert! Horaaaaaah!!!"